PUFFIN BOOKS
Under the Autumn Garden

It was half-term, and Mrs Collinge wanted her pupils
to find out all they could about the history of their part
of Norfolk. Any interesting things that they found
would be put in a little museum at school.

Matthew, was head boy, so he felt he had to do
something really good. Simply finding out the date of
his house was too ordinary. But people said his family's
garden lay over the remains of an old priory.

But what would he find if he did start digging? The
search didn't turn out in the least as Matthew had
planned. The builder's children kept getting in the way
and turning his excavations into play-houses. Then Mrs
Collinge kept demanding written work when Matthew
was still only digging, and the people next door were
always worrying when their cats got lost. So he wasn't
finding out much, not even about the local ghost, Sir
Oliver, who was said to come clanking by in full
armour every November. It looked very much as if the
search was a waste of time, until the tide suddenly
turned.

Jan Mark is one of today's most highly acclaimed
writers for the young, having won the Carnegie Medal
twice for *Thunder and Lightnings* (1976) and *Handles*
(1983). She lives with her family in the Norfolk village
of Ingham.

Other books by Jan Mark

UNDER THE
AUTUMN GARDEN

Jan Mark

Puffin Books

Puffin Books, Penguin Books Ltd, Harmondsworth, Middlesex, England
Viking Penguin Inc., 40 West 23rd Street, New York, New York 10010, U.S.A.
Penguin Books Australia Ltd, Ringwood, Victoria, Australia
Penguin Books Canada Limited, 2801 John Street, Markham, Ontario, Canada L3R 1B4
Penguin Books (N.Z.) Ltd, 182–190 Wairau Road, Auckland 10, New Zealand

First published by Kestrel Books 1977
Published in Puffin Books 1980
Reprinted 1984, 1987

Made and printed in Great Britain by
Richard Clay Ltd, Bungay, Suffolk
Set in Monotype Baskerville

For my mother

Contents

1. Ship Loke and Myhill Street

'I'll write to you,' said Matthew.

'Bet you forget,' said Darren.

'I will,' said Matthew. 'I've got the address here, some-where.'

'Bet you lose it,' said Darren, as Matthew began patting all his pockets in turn. 'Hang on, I've got something for you. Better not lose this.' From his lapel he unpinned the badge with Head Boy printed on it and handed it to Matthew.

'Put that on,' he said. 'Let's see how you look.'

Matthew took the blue and white badge and pinned it on his sweater.

'Very nice,' said Darren. 'You won't like that, though.'

'What won't I like?' One thing about Darren that Matthew wouldn't miss was Darren's mania for arguments. He could never hear a statement without turning it over and worrying at it, like a cat with a frog.

'Being Head Boy,' said Darren. 'You think you will at first, but in the end you'll wish that it wasn't you. Every-one'll look at you different once you've got that on.'

'But I won't be different,' said Matthew. He had been Darren's lieutenant since September and all the time envied him the seven short days that made Darren the elder, and therefore Head Boy until he left. Now Darren was going into hospital and Matthew was Head Boy in his place.

'That's only for a month, remember,' said Darren, in case Matthew developed ideas above his station.

They closed the iron gates of the school playground and walked to the corner. Matthew wheeled his bike. Darren limped.

'What's up with your leg?' asked Matthew.

'I'm going to be operated on, aren't I?' said Darren.

'I thought that was your ear.'

'No one can see if there's anything wrong with an ear,' said Darren. 'You can't limp with that. Anyway, that makes me ache all down one side, just thinking about it.'

'You'll miss all that history we've got to do.'

'I'll miss half term, too,' said Darren.

'No you won't. Half term's this Monday and Tuesday.'

'Well, they're carving me up on Monday, that won't feel like half term,' said Darren, sashaying across the road as his limp went out of control. Matthew mounted his bike.

'See you then,' he said, out of habit.

'No you won't.'

'I'll write.'

'Bet you don't.'

The limp became a quickstep, then a gallop and he skidded round the corner, out of sight, leaving Matthew to ride home alone.

Home past the recreation ground and the churchyard, where the moles were stirring; home past the pigsties, past the dell where the bluebells and the gas stoves grew.

Matthew stopped here to finish the chewing gum that Darren had lent him. It was banned at home since the time he had left a piece on the dresser and it had got onto the sole plate of the iron. He could still see Dad's shirt and the steaming strings.

The dell was shaded by trees and in spring, when the bluebells were in flower, the new, broad, sycamore leaves hid the bottom of the dell from view. Today, halfway through the autumn term and halfway through the long, downhill run towards Christmas, he could just see the five abandoned gas stoves, four standing and one lying, on last year's leaves at the foot of the slope. By the end of term, this year's leaves would have joined them and the stoves would be in full view from the road above, where he stood with his bicycle.

He rolled the chewing gum into a ball and cast it down among the leaves, watching it bounce and bury itself. A car drew up behind him and a voice said, 'Have you lost something?' It was Mrs Bagnall, who owned six cats and lived in a bungalow at Myhill Street, near Matthew's house. She was a teacher at the secondary school in Polthorpe, where Matthew would be going next year when he was eleven. At the moment she was a good friend: next year she would be too close for comfort. Mr Bagnall was a teacher too, but further off, so he didn't count.

'I was looking at the gas stoves,' said Matthew, nodding towards the dell.

'Disgraceful,' said Mrs Bagnall. 'When we first moved here there was only one of them and a bucket. I don't know how the rest get down there without someone seeing them arrive. They must be breeding. I notice someone has slung an oil-drum in our pond. If I catch him at it again I'll send him in after it, head first.'

She drove on and Matthew followed. From the dell the road ran on a shallow slope to the corner of Fen Street, then climbed again towards Myhill Street, the cluster of houses round Ship Loke, which was where Matthew lived.

On the way he passed the pond where the oil-drum had been left. It was only a pond in winter. In summer it was a green hollow, bearded with rushes, where Mrs Bagnall's cats lurked and hunted. For Matthew, it was the first sign of winter when the pond began to fill with water.

By the time he reached the bungalow Mrs Bagnall had gone indoors, and her car stood in the garage. He turned left, into Ship Loke. The corner house belonged to Mrs Harrison and she was in her garden, sweeping away dead leaves with a birch broom. When she saw Matthew she waved the broom over the gate to bring him to a halt.

'I see you're going to have company,' she said, as he stopped. She pointed with the broom to the next house. It was the one that was joined to Matthew's house and it had been empty for years. It now belonged to Dad, who was going to have the two buildings knocked into one. Since Matthew left home that morning, someone had planted a wooden notice board in the hedge: GEO. ANGEL BUILDER AND DECORATOR.

'Your Dad's not wasting any time,' said Mrs Harrison.

'He wants to get the roof done before winter,' said Matthew, turning to look at Mrs Harrison while he spoke. She was slightly deaf and had to be able to see what he was saying, but he didn't have to shout. She had more trouble with the Bagnalls. They made a great effort to speak carefully but they came from another part of the country and used differently shaped words.

'Why are we going to have company?' asked Matthew, but Mrs Harrison had turned back to her sweeping and didn't see him speak. He went on, past the sign and into his own garden where Mum was digging potatoes behind the garage.

'How's the Head Boy, then?' said Mum.

'Just about the same as he was at lunch time,' said Matthew, propping his bike against the wall. Mum lifted her basket of potatoes and followed him indoors. She seldom had to ask him what went on at school because she was the school dinner lady. The food came, already cooked, from the big school in Polthorpe, but Mum, in a white cap and overall, was there each day to warm the plates, serve the meals, and wash up afterwards.

She tipped the potatoes into the kitchen sink and gave Matthew the basket to take outside.

'I'll put the kettle on,' she said. 'Were you surprised when they said it would be you?'

'Not really,' said Matthew. 'I'm the oldest one there, now. Anne Lilley's the next one after me. She'll have her turn next year. Anyway, that only means I'm in charge of the milk bottles.'

It meant very much more than that for the Head Person had to keep an eye on things without anyone noticing that it was being done. He also had to behave slightly better than anyone else. Taking charge of the milk bottles was only a sign of office; a rare but useless privilege that singled you out as being the only one worthy to enjoy it.

'Mrs Harrison said we were going to have company,' said Matthew. 'What did she mean?'

'How would she know?' said Mum.

'Did she mean Mr Angel?'

'I suppose you could call him company,' said Mum. 'But he'll be up on the roof, most of the time. You're not going up there with him,' she added.

Mr Angel was a builder. He lived in the next village but he kept his lorries at the yard in Polthorpe. They were a familiar sight and exactly the colour of an Edam cheese. They were painted yellow with rind-red lettering: Geo. Angel. Builder and decorator. Matthew liked cheese but he could never fancy Edam. It tasted of brick dust and rubble and just seeing it on the shelf in the supermarket made his tongue feel gritty.

Dad came home early on Fridays, had a special, large Friday tea, and then went back to work late at his garage. When he came in he dropped a bunch of keys on the table.

'You'd better hang those up somewhere, Janey, and give them to George when he come,' he said. 'I see he've been round already, by the sign. You'll be having company, Matthew.'

'Mrs Harrison said that,' said Matthew. 'Who's the company?'

Mum picked the keys out of the jam, wiped them on a dishcloth and hung them on a nail behind the door.

'George bring his boys with him at weekends,' said Dad. 'One of them's about your age.'

'That'll make up for Darren being away,' said Mum. Matthew saw other possibilities, not all of them good.

'Julie and Karen won't come will they?'

Julie and Karen Angel went to Matthew's school. Their father was Mr John Angel, George's brother and junior partner.

'What's wrong with Julie and Karen?' asked Mum, who only saw them at lunch-time when they were eating; something they did well.

'Karen tells tales,' said Matthew. 'And Julie nags. She's never happy unless she's mobbing someone. She goes on, whaa-whaa-whaa, just like a chain saw.' He thought about Julie for a bit. 'She'll have to do what I say now, won't she?'

'I wouldn't bet on that,' said Mum, pushing his duffel bag to one side to make room for the tea. 'You don't want to come down too heavy to begin with.'

'She never bothered Darren,' said Matthew. 'He wouldn't let her, but I don't know how he did it. I should have asked him before he went.'

'I made bread today,' said Mum. 'Get a new loaf out of the bin. You don't want to be like Darren. Just be Matthew, only better.'

Mum had never had much time for Darren.

'When's Mr Angel going to start?' asked Matthew.

'Next week, I hope,' said Dad. 'You never know with George. You can take a note over to Hoxenham tomorrow, Matthew, to remind him we're still here. He might think he've done his bit, else, just putting the sign up.'

'Why not phone him?' asked Mum. 'Who wants more tea?'

'I do,' said Dad, holding out his Friday teacup which was as big as the sugar basin. 'Don't never phone George up, Janey, unless that's life and death. He'll chat all day if you let him. If he want to do that on his own phone bill, he's welcome, but he's not doing that on ours.'

'Can I go and look at the house?' said Matthew. 'I won't touch anything.'

'You'd better not,' said Dad. 'You'll have the whole place down round your ears if you breathe too heavy. Go on, I'll be round myself in a minute, when I've had another cup.' He took the Friday teacup, poured the tea down his throat in a single cataract and pushed the cup towards the teapot again.

He clearly had a busy evening ahead of him.

2. In a Glass, Darkly

The house next door had a name instead of a number. It was painted in frayed but dashing gold letters on the glass panel over the front door: Kingston Villa. Matthew wondered if Dad intended to take over the name along with the house. It was too grand a name for such a modest front door but with the two small houses made into one it might be a better fit.

Kingston Villa sounded more impressive than 3, Ship Loke. It would look nice in the school register too, between Lilley, Anne Patricia, Oak Cottage and Oulton, Stephen Robert John, Railway Farm, which was a lie in any case because the railway had gone, long ago. He tried it for size: Marsh, Matthew, Kingston Villa, Ship Loke, Myhill Street. It had a good rolling sound and it was far more address than anyone else had, especially if you added Pallingham, Norfolk. It quite made up for having less name.

He turned the key in the lock and went in. Standing at the foot of the stairs he could see that it was identical to his own house only back to front, as if seen in a dirty mirror. All the same rooms were there, but on the right instead of the left, and decorated with green grime and cobwebs instead of wallpaper and plaster.

In the kitchen there was no sink, only a lone tap lagged in tattered sacking like a snake with a sore throat. Where Mum had her shining gas cooker there lurked a black range, still full of ash, and the floor was laid with pamments instead of the black and white tiles that they had at home. Matthew knew that under the pamments there was nothing but cold earth and the chill rose up through the very soles of his shoes as he stood in the dank and darkening kitchen, so much darker than his, although the same low October sun that shone on Mum and Dad at the tea table was shining in here, also.

He wrote 'Kilroy was here' in the dust on the window, back to front so that it could be read outside, and drew a face with ravenous teeth, underneath it. Then he went back through the hall, past the long-dead telephone, and into the front garden. Dad was standing at the gate, staring up at the roof.

'That's a horrible sight,' he said. 'We'll have to strip the lot. God knows what's nesting up there. If Joe Blakely had sold six years ago, when I first wanted to buy, that wouldn't be in this mess now. He always was a silly old fool about parting with anything. I reckon he pulled down his greenhouse in case he grew more than he could eat and had to give the stuff away.'

The Blakelys had moved into Kingston Villa before Matthew was born and had moved out again before he was old enough to remember them, but Mum and Dad, and Mrs Harrison, still spoke of the amazing events that followed their arrival. They had cut down all the fruit trees, pulled up all the flowers and let the grass grow. Grass was all that grew there now. There had once been three sheds and a greenhouse but Mr Joe Blakely, assisted by his two sons and watched by his wife, had razed them to the ground and buried them.

'I went round there,' said Dad, 'and offered to buy the lot, but he weren't having any. They laid everything on the ground and jumped up and down, the three of them, until that was all little pieces. Then they dug a big hole and buried the bits. Mrs B. had a hammer, she took care of the glass. And not one of them ever said a word. Just jumped up and down all afternoon, till there was nothing left. I tell you, your mother never felt properly safe while they was here. That were a long five years.'

The Blakelys had gone away at last but they still owned the house and it had stood empty ever since. Matthew joined Dad at the gate and looked up as well. On the Marshes' side the roof was flat and neat, the pantiles snugly interlocking. The tiles on Kingston Villa were bulging and rickety, the roof like a quilt thrown over an unmade bed.

'Oh dear, oh dear,' said Dad, sorrowfully. 'George is going to be busy.'

Matthew was not encouraged to call Mr Angel 'George', but Dad, who serviced his lorries at the garage, called him George and a number of other things besides, especially when he was working on the engines.

'And that's not only the roof,' said Dad, as they walked round the side of the house. 'There's some bad things in those front bedrooms. That surveyor bloke looked quite poorly when he came out of the airing cupboard.' He thumped the wall of the lean-to as they went by. Flakes and splinters fell from the eaves. 'Don't you go leaning on anything, we might have an accident on our hands.' They turned the corner of the house, into the back garden. 'And that hedge is coming down, too.'

Dad went back to work but Matthew walked down the new garden, through the gathering evening, to the wall. This was the middle section of a wall that ran along the end of Matthew's garden and ended at the Hoxenham Road, passing between the gardens of Mrs Harrison and the Bagnalls, on the way. It was part of a much higher wall, all that was left of a thirteenth-century priory, according to local maps, where it said Priory (remains of) in crooked black letters, to indicate great age.

There was no priory now, and no remains, except for the flint wall which someone, long ago, had levelled off with bricks.

Matthew leaned on the bricks and gazed at his new view of

Hemp's Farm and its fields, and the footpath that passed through them, across Fen Street and up to the church. He sometimes used it to get to school and in a way it was his path because every autumn Charlie Hemp ploughed over it and whoever first used the footpath after that, set its course for the whole year. Matthew always tried to be the first because it was very difficult to walk in a straight line over ploughland and the footpath came out with interesting kinks in it. It gave him a powerful feeling to look down the path as he was doing now, and see the kinks still there, and to know that they were of his own making, endorsed by the feet of all the other people who used the path.

It would soon be time for ploughing again. Already the gangster gulls were gathering daily in the rotting stubble that had lain there since Charlie cut his wheat and spread muck, back in September.

November began tomorrow and Matthew, leaning on the twilight wall, recalled that with November came Sir Oliver, when he might be seen again on the footpath. Sir Oliver, if he had ever lived, had died in the fevery fogs of a medieval autumn, and in the season of his death he could yet be seen, stomping, as only a knight in full armour could stomp, down the slope from Pallingham church, and up to Myhill Street.

Sir Oliver must surely be the most boring ghost in the county. Other Broadland villages boasted flaming monks, headless horsemen, phantom coaches, and, excessively, an entire Roman legion. Pallingham had only Sir Oliver, trudging glumly up and down the footpath like any law-abiding citizen.

Matthew knew of no one who had ever seen him, which rendered him even more boring.

The only person likely to was Charlie Hemp, ploughing his fields by night. Matthew meant to ask him, this year, if the lights of the tractor had picked out the figure of Sir Oliver, clanking silently up the field ahead of him.

3. Eggs and Angels

Mrs Sadler was the school playground supervisor and lived on the Calstead Road, just beyond the school, with her mother-in-law and two dozen hens. The hens belonged to old Mrs Sadler and every Saturday Matthew made his usual weekday journey, only this time to buy eggs. There was a sign in the garden to trap casual passers-by, who had to make their way between the hen runs to the front door, but Mrs Sadler kept a supply for her regular customers in a shed near the gate. As well as his own, Matthew collected eggs for Mrs Harrison and Mrs Bagnall, delivering them on the way home.

When he called at the bungalow no one answered his knock, and he was just about to leave the eggs on the step when he saw Mr Bagnall in the garden, pulling up turnips. He was very scientific about it, taking hold of each turnip and gently unwinding it. If it failed to come up in his hand he wound it up again and left it in the earth.

Matthew was a little nervous of Mr Bagnall. He had a dislocated look, as if all his bones were threaded on cotton, and he professed to have a great hatred of cats. Matthew found it embarrassing to see Mrs Bagnall petting her cats while her husband scowled at them and made unfriendly remarks. Mrs Bagnall took no notice at all and occasionally added another cat to the collection, even as Mr Bagnall was threatening to slay all the others. They seemed quite fond of each other, in all other respects, but Matthew often feared that a row would break out involving both Bagnalls and all the cats.

'I've brought the eggs,' he said, to Mr Bagnall. 'They're on the doorstep.'

Two cats who were scrapping in the apple tree fell out of the branches, thudding to the ground like ripe fruit.

'Disgusting creatures,' said Mr Bagnall. 'Infecting the trees with their poisonous whiskers.'

One of the cats swore and ran up a tree trunk. The other undulated against Mr Bagnall's ankles.

'She likes you,' said Matthew. 'She's purring.'

'Nonsense,' said Mr Bagnall, with a cruel, rasping noise, as if he had gravel in his throat. 'She's charging up her death rays.'

'The eggs are on the step,' said Matthew, again, and hurried back to the road. Sometimes it seemed as if Mr Bagnall must be joking, but as he never smiled it was hard to tell. When he reached his bicycle, Minnie, the smallest of the six, was sitting in the carrier, on Mrs Harrison's eggs.

'Come you out of that,' said Matthew, hurriedly removing her. 'He'll pull all your legs off, he always says he will.' He stroked the little cat under the chin and she pushed her head against his face. Mr Bagnall also claimed that cats had nothing inside their heads except a damp passage, from ear to ear, along which the wind whistled continuously.

As Matthew turned the corner into Ship Loke, Dad passed him in the Land-Rover, on his way to work.

'Don't you forget that message,' said Dad, leaning out of the window.

'What message?'

'You have forgot. Where did you leave your head?' said Dad. 'The message for George. I gave that to your Mum to give to you. Remember to ask her for it.'

He drove away. Matthew delivered Mrs Harrison's eggs

and went home where breakfast and the message were waiting for him.

Ship Loke lay on the parish boundary. Myhill Street was in the parish of Pallingham but the loke was bordered by a shaggy hedge, leading down to the woods, and this was the boundary. On the other side was Hoxenham. The village itself was out of sight behind trees but it was not far away and going in a straight line Matthew could have reached it in five minutes. However, the road had elbows so it took three times longer to reach even the centre of the village, and Mr Angel lived on the far side of the broad, much further on. He rode through the village along the edge of the broad where the boats, abandoned by summer visitors, rocked on the still water, disturbed by the slightest movement of wind or water fowl. Ahead was the deserted road, fenced by alder and willow, with nothing on either side of it but marshland and water.

He had travelled in a semicircle since leaving home and looking across the broad he could just see the elms that stood at the end of Ship Loke. Myhill Street was not only on the edge of the parish, it was on the edge of the land drains. On all sides the dykes and ditches stretched away towards the grimlie length of Hoxenham Wall, the biggest dyke of all. In winter it might well have been on the edge of the world: nothing between Norfolk and outer space but the bleached reeds. They stood everywhere, dry and coldly whispering.

Just as he was beginning to think that he had taken a wrong turning he saw a notice, half hidden by the bulk of a collapsing willow tree: Geo. Angel. Builder and decorator.

A similar notice stood in the Angels' yard at Polthorpe, but this was Mr Angel's house. Matthew wheeled the bike up the drive and stared about him. The scenery inside the garden was the same as the scenery outside. All the bleakness of the marshes enclosed by a hedge. It was not so much a garden as an estate.

There were two or three buildings that looked as though they might be lived in, besides the rusty iron sheds, nissen huts, hen houses and prefabricated garages that stood about the grounds. A scabby dinosaur leaned out of the bushes as he went by. It was a derelict combine harvester, one of the many wrecks that skulked in the undergrowth. For a master builder, Mr Angel seemed to lead a ramshackle existence.

The drive took him to the largest building, an old house, much added to, with an asbestos garage tacked on at one side. Matthew could hear scraping sounds from somewhere but although a car stood in the garage with its bonnet raised he couldn't see anyone. He went to the nearest door and knocked, wondering whether it was the front or the back door. No one opened it and he waited on the step, considering what to do with the message; there was no letter-box. He stepped out of the porch and listened carefully. The scraping sounds were definitely coming from the garage, as if the car was scratching itself. He stood in the doorway and called 'Anybody there?'

He had a nasty shock.

Two clutching hands appeared from under the car, between the front wheels. For a moment he thought there had been a horrible accident, then he saw an oily face behind the hands.

'Hullo,' said the face.

Matthew bent down and saw that the face belonged to someone who was crouched in an inspection pit under the car.

'I've got a message for Mr Angel,' he said, upside down, to the face.

'Hold on,' said the face and retired to the end of the pit. Matthew heard clambering and the owner of the face appeared from behind the rear of the car.

'Which Mr Angel is it for?' he asked, from a great height. Matthew wondered how he managed to fit into the inspection pit. Perhaps he had extra joints and hinges that shorter people like Matthew could do without.

'Mr George,' he said, looking at the envelope to make sure. Apart from Julie's father, Mr John, he hadn't known about any others. 'Which Mr Angel are you?'

'I'm Chris. You want my father but he's out on a roof in Tokesby. Or do you want Grandad? He's George as well, over there.' He pointed to a green, corrugated iron bungalow on the other side of the estate.

'I want your Dad,' said Matthew. 'It's from my Dad, Mr Marsh. He services your lorries.'

'Now I know you,' said Chris. 'Give that to me, I'll see he gets it.' He leaned forward and took the note in his teeth, waving black hands to show why he couldn't hold it. He spoke through clenched jaws. 'Would you open the door for me?'

Matthew went back to the house and opened the door. It led straight into a shining bathroom, all tiles and chromium plate, with a thick carpet on the floor.

'Mustn't touch anything,' said Chris, still mumbling. 'We've only just finished it. Turn on the taps, will you?' His voice vibrated through the note like a wasp in a jam jar.

Matthew approached the sink with respect and turned on the taps. He had never been in a bathroom that opened straight on to the garden; it was a draughty thought. Chris was removing his boots on the doorstep.

'You'd better take your letter back,' he said. 'I might chew it, by mistake.'

Matthew withdrew the note and returned it to his pocket.

'This used to be the scullery,' said Chris, scooping green jelly from a tin under the sink and larding his arms with it. 'We've been working at it since Christmas, on and off. Got to get that door bricked up, yet.'

'My Dad uses that stuff to shift grease,' said Matthew.

24

'He gets it by the gallon. That's much cheaper than those little tins.'

'Do you think he'd get me some?' said Chris. 'Very handy, working in a garage.'

'He owns it,' said Matthew. 'Half of it, anyway. Do you work in a garage?'

'I'm still at school,' said Chris, rinsing his arms and beginning on his face. As the dirt came off Matthew saw that he was quite a bit younger than he had seemed at first. He began to look like a schoolboy except for the peaty side-whiskers that remained round his ears after the rest of the black had gone. 'I hope to go to London, next year.'

'To work in a garage?' Matthew put a towel into Chris's groping hand.

'No, to the university, to read History,' said Chris, coming out of the towel. 'Where's that note? I'm sure to lose it.'

'You gave that back to me. Don't lose it,' said Matthew. 'Dad'll think I forgot to bring it. That's all about our roof, that needs mending.'

'I won't really lose it,' said Chris. He started to leave the room by a second door. Matthew thought that he had better follow as he still had the note.

'It's a bind,' said Chris, 'remembering to lock all these doors every time you want to use the loo.'

Matthew looked back and noticed a third door, behind the bath.

'Coal-shed,' said Chris.

The door they were using led into the living-room. Chris walked on, opened another door and they were outside again, looking towards the green bungalow.

'The note,' said Matthew, waving it at Chris.

'Yes. Thanks,' said Chris, taking it. He looked distracted. 'What's that whistling noise?'

'Like a siren?'

'Cistern's overflowing,' said Chris. He returned the note

to Matthew and dived into the house again. Matthew waited in the doorway and looked around. The house seemed to have fallen apart and been carelessly reassembled without regard for the original design. At the end of the room a flight of stairs stopped abruptly where it met the ceiling and under the wallpaper he could see the outlines of a door. Perhaps Mr Angel practised building on his own house to save spoiling other people's. By the time he had finished with Kingston Villa it might have staircases that emerged airily from the roof, and all the windows underground.

Chris came back with wet hair.

'That's seen to,' he said, strolling away. Matthew still had the note. He ran after him.

'What was that you said about reading history?' he asked, catching him up. 'We've got to do history this term.'

'I have to do it all the time,' said Chris.

'So do we,' said Matthew. 'But this is special. We've got to find all the history in our village. I don't know where to look. That's all fields.'

'You'll have to look under them. Turn archaeologist,' said Chris. 'You live at Myhill Street, don't you? You've got the priory there.'

'Not any more,' said Matthew. 'That's only there on the map. You can't see anything.'

'Well, then, like I said; you'll have to dig for it,' said Chris. 'Hullo, here comes the mob.'

Round the side of the bungalow ran Julie and Karen, followed by a very little boy dressed in denim and dirt, waving a red plastic sword.

Julie's round face became long and quarrelsome when she saw Matthew. She stopped running and approached him.

'What are you doing here, Matthew Marsh?' said Julie.

'Matthew Marsh, Luke and John,' said Karen. It was either a greeting or an insult and coming from Karen that made very little difference. He had heard it many times.

'We've come to see our Nanny and Grandad. We don't want to see you,' said Julie.

'I don't want to see you, either,' said Matthew.

'Clive hit me with his sword,' said Karen.

'Don't hit Karen with your sword, Clive,' said Chris.

'Is torque wrench,' growled Clive and hit Matthew instead.

'You don't have to hit me either,' said Matthew, rather impressed that Clive should know what a torque wrench looked like.

'You can't tell him what to do,' said Julie. 'You don't start being Head Boy till Wednesday. You can't tell him what to do anyway. Chris will hit you.'

This seemed highly unlikely.

Clive made an aimless swipe at everybody and plunged into the bushes, revving-up as he went. He seemed to be about three years old but he sounded as though he smoked heavily.

'Matthew's a loony,' said Karen, for want of something more appropriate to say.

In the distance Matthew saw someone else erupt from the green bungalow and head towards them.

'Matthew's a loony, a poony, a goony, a moony, a foony,' droned Karen, elaborating on her original theme. Faced with a seemingly endless supply of Angels from the bungalow, he handed the note back to Chris.

'I'd better get home now,' he said, and went.

The cries of the Angels faded into the distance as he pedalled down the road. He took the track that led out past the Slepe Bridge draining pump and into the Marrams, the dunes that bordered the coast. He didn't look back as he left the bike at the foot of the dunes and climbed up, through Slepe Gap, and down onto the beach. The sands and the sea were empty: he walked down to the edge of the water and sat there, letting the buzz go out of his ears. A little fat dog minced along the sand, glanced at Matthew and sat down a few yards away, courteously looking out to sea instead of grinning at him, after the fashion of solitary dogs. After a while it got up and walked quietly away. He was almost sorry to see it go.

It was such a gentlemanly dog.

4. Hare Today

Charlie Hemp had a freezer into which went everything that he shot: hares, rabbits, pigeons and ducks. Since he lived alone and shot more than he could eat he sorted through it once a month and distributed meat amongst his friends.

'What's this, then?' asked Dad, looking at the frosty carcase on the draining board.

'A hare,' said Mum.

'That's what he tell you,' said Dad. 'One of these days we're going to get a fox by mistake.'

Mum put the hare in a casserole and went out to do some gardening while it cooked. She knelt on a raft of sacking in the middle of the flower bed, digging up roots, while Matthew was set to pick up the rotting windfalls that remained under the apple trees. If they lay until spring the pips sprouted and little trees began to grow.

'Didn't Mrs Collinge give you any work over the holiday?' asked Mum, tossing weeds into the grass box from the mower.

'Sort of,' said Matthew. 'She wants us to think about something.'

'She'll be lucky,' said Mum. 'Or did she tell you what to think about?'

Matthew sat back on his heels and practised aiming apples at the grass box. They struck the curving metal with soft, fruity explosions. 'You know that festival they're having in Polthorpe, next Easter? All the schools are doing a history of their village to put on show in the Town Hall. We're going to do one.'

'I heard about that,' said Mum. 'Is that your work then?'

'We've got to start by finding out about our own houses and when they were built, and what they're built of.'

'That shouldn't take long,' said Mum. 'You'd better get on with it.'

'That's so boring.' Matthew looked up at the house. He had lived in it all his life. Writing about it would be as entertaining as writing a history of his knees: it was part of him. 'I could do the priory.'

'Do what? That's all gone,' said Mum. 'I think I'll go and look at that hare – that smells about done to me.'

'There's Sir Oliver,' said Matthew. 'He's still here.'

Mum stood up and stamped the loose earth from her shoes.

'He's only a story. You don't want to write about him.'

'He was real once,' said Matthew. 'He must have been. You have to be dead to be a ghost and you can't be dead unless you've been alive. He goes up and down to the priory so he must think there's something there.' Even if you don't, he said to himself.

'Don't go wasting time with a silly ghost story,' said Mum. 'You've got to go back and do some real hard work, on Wednesday. You don't want to get wrong, now you're Head Boy.' She went indoors.

Matthew occasionally got tired of hearing about what he did and didn't want to do. He had his own ideas about that. He took the grass box down to the wall, emptied it on the rubbish heap and stood, looking down the footpath. He had the beginnings of an idea, of the slow-growing variety. Dad strolled across the garden but Matthew didn't notice him. Dad waggled his fingers in front of Matthew's eyes to attract his attention.

'Wake up,' he said. 'What are you doing, asleep on your feet?'

'I was thinking,' said Matthew.

'Not like you,' said Dad.

Matthew sighed, but silently. People seemed to have a very low opinion of his thoughts: Mum, Dad and Mrs Collinge. Dad lit his pipe and the smoke mingled with the smell of the baked hare. It was an amiable moment, a good time to mention his idea. He approached the subject in a general sort of way.

'Do you know when they're coming to do the roof?' he asked.

'George rang up this morning,' said Dad. 'Said he'd just found my note, stuck behind the clock. Who did you say you gave it to?'

This was not a very promising start.

'I gave that to Chris. He was the only one I could find,' said Matthew.

'Oh, him. If he got his head out of a car for five minutes his brains might settle,' said Dad. 'When I get their Volvo in I spend more time repairing his repairs than I would if he'd let that alone. George said they might be over tomorrow. That might mean tomorrow, you never know with George.'

It was sooner than he had expected.

'What's going to happen about the garden?'

'Plenty of time to think of that, later,' said Dad. 'We'll have the hedge down first, then we'll get the foul-grass out and dig up the roots. Are you making me an offer?'

Matthew looked across at the hedge. The foul-grass sneaked out of the garden beyond, wound itself round the bottom of the hedge and climbed into the twigs, where it fixed itself as tight as ivy. It was a privet hedge.

'If you get rid of that hedge I shan't have anything to feed my stick-insects on.'

'Never mind them,' said Dad, who thought that stick-insects were unnatural. 'Every time Charlie have his culti-vator out that fill up with dust. That's a sieve, that hedge. I

31

daresay Mrs Bagnall will let you have a bit of privet now and again. Well, are you going to help?'

'Oh, yes,' said Matthew, wondering how he could get out of it. 'I was thinking about digging, too.'

'That'll be a while before I start digging,' said Dad. 'I'll have to go over the grass first, with a scythe. I don't fancy you let loose with a scythe,' he added, looking down sideways at Matthew. 'What are you after?'

'I want to dig up the garden,' said Matthew. 'I want to see what's underneath.'

'Three sheds and a greenhouse,' said Dad. 'And that's just for starters. If I said there was everything bar the kitchen sink down there I'd be lying because the kitchen sink's there too. I saw them bury that. I suppose they meant to put a new one in, but they never did. Why don't you dig up our garden? I could do with a hand, this autumn.'

Matthew knew when he was being cornered.

'There's this thing we're doing at school. Mrs Collinge wants us to find out about history and how old our houses are. We're going to make a little museum out of all the bits we find.'

'I reckon that will be little,' said Dad. 'What do you expect to find here? You're not going to put old Blakely's greenhouse in a museum, I suppose?'

'I thought I might dig up the priory,' said Matthew. He didn't want to tell anyone about his idea, but if he didn't he might find himself digging the vegetable plot, all autumn.

'You won't find much priory, I can tell you,' said Dad. 'Don't you think Charlie would have had something up, by now?'

Mum leaned out of the kitchen window and called 'Come and get washed. That'll be ready in five minutes.'

Dad went straight indoors but Matthew collected the tools and put them away. Mum wouldn't feel like gardening after lunch.

*

'That's your turn to wash up,' said Mum, when they had finished eating.

'That's always our turn to wash up,' said Dad.

'That's always my turn to cook. You do the cooking and I'll wash up.'

'Now, about this here priory,' said Dad, when they were washing up as usual. 'I don't reckon you'll find anything but you're welcome to look. All I say is this: you can take out what you like, but don't you dare put anything in. There must be enough rubbish under that grass to build another house with.'

Matthew hung up the tea towels to dry and ran outside. He went down the garden, through the gap where the hedge met the wall, and surfaced in the long grass that would have been hay if anyone had cut it. The hollow stems were battered and flattened, lying in yellow rags.

It was the wrong time of day for Sir Oliver but Matthew closed his eyes and saw him like a photographic negative, black where he should have been white, and furry at the edges. Sir Oliver trembled and dissolved and he saw monks, solid and solemn as they appeared in his history book at school. He had once met a real monk in Norwich, wearing glasses and walking briskly through the bus station with a brief-case in his hand; no more than a business man out in his dressing-gown.

What would he find if he did dig? What did monks do in those far-off days before they walked abroad, catching buses?

Monks prayed in their priory. He saw a church packed with bowed bald heads like hazel-nuts; a church with its roof gone, with its walls gone, a grassy mound embedded with stones and the monks gone; then the mound assaulted by men with spades, digging; himself digging; himself at school, face to face with Mrs Collinge, displaying the things he had found.

What had he found?

He opened his eyes and he was face to face with Mrs Bagnall's tabby cat, a swaggering tom tiger who had started life as a kitten called Skippy but was now known as Genghis Khan, because of his nasty habits.

Genghis Khan was taking home a rat to put away for later. He lounged past Matthew and slithered over the wall.

'Loathsome beast,' said Mr Bagnall, in the distance.

Matthew switched off the pictures and looked about him. Nearby lay a manhole cover, like a big iron biscuit thrown out for the birds. He pushed it to one side and there was no manhole under it but it had been there so long that the earth beneath was bare of plants. It was the one place where he could begin digging without waiting for the grass to be cut. He went home and fetched the edging spade from the toolshed. Dad came in as he went out.

'Where are you going with that?'

'I'm going to start digging.'

'The priory?'

'Yes,' said Matthew. Dad laughed.

'Well, that's all right for a bit of fun, I suppose, but mind that is just for fun. You do something else for your school work, and do it properly.'

'Oh, yes,' said Matthew. 'Yes. Yes.' Dad would tell Mum and Mum would tell Mrs Collinge. He must keep a set of false papers for school and pretend that the excavation was only a game until he found something and astounded them all.

He took the spade back to the new garden and drove it into the earth. There was no question of digging in earnest until the grass was cut, but he had begun. This was where the excavation would be.

5. Owl in the Moon

He meant to make an early start on Monday morning. There was no one about when he went through the hedge to the new garden carrying the spade and the shears. A slight breeze stirred the trees and dry leaves fell from the oak with the rattle of distant applause. In Mrs Bagnall's garden the chestnut leaves, yellow as bananas, coasted to the ground with a soft slapping sound.

The oak was the only tree that the Blakelys had failed to cut down. Driven aslant by centuries of storms, it leaned across the garden; its branches grabbing at the house, its roots under the wall. As Matthew stood by it he heard a louder rattle and saw a tractor approaching up the field. Charlie had begun his ploughing, attended by his officious black Labrador retriever.

The dog was called Yew, after Charlie's uncle. Written down it was actually Hugh, but as the uncle was dead and the dog couldn't write, it didn't matter very much. Yew was supposed to be a gun dog but Charlie, who was very firm about cats, rats, and rabbits, was soft on dogs so Yew ran about with a wild white smile, often in the wrong direction, and brought back the pigeons that Charlie shot squashed flat in his jaws.

Matthew waved to Charlie as he turned at the top of the field, and Yew fell into a noisy panic, trying to decide if he should investigate Matthew or follow the tractor. Already the first gulls were assembling in the furrows and they scattered angrily as the dog cantered among them. Matthew turned his attention to the excavation. He took the shears first and knelt in the damp grass to cut back the growth round the hole that he had dug yesterday. After a few minutes he felt that someone was watching him and looking up he saw Mrs Harrison leaning over the fence.

'Wrong time of year for that,' she said.

'I'm not gardening,' said Matthew. 'Just digging a hole.'

'That can't have been dug for eleven years, you'll need a pickaxe. You can't dig a hole with shears,' said Mrs Harrison.

'I'm just cutting the grass so I can see where to dig,' said Matthew. He tried to add a little dignity to the situation. 'I'm looking for the priory.' It sounded extremely silly, said to Mrs Harrison, but silly enough to seem like a game and that was a means of preserving his secret.

'Doing that for school are you?' asked Mrs Harrison. No secret: Mum had been telling tales. Now that Mrs Harrison was next door instead of next door but one she could do it in comfort without raising her voice.

'Not really,' said Matthew, as casually as he could. 'That was the school thing that gave me the idea, that's all. I might find something.' Mrs Harrison walked down to her section of the wall and motioned him to do the same on his side of the fence.

'That's the priory, down there,' she said, pointing to Charlie's stubble. 'That's where you ought to be digging.'

'I can't dig up Charlie's field. Anyway, they wouldn't have buried monks in the priory, would they? Didn't they have to do that outside?'

'Oh, you want to dig up people, do you?' said Mrs Harrison. 'I remember when they had the archaeologists at Clipton. They were digging all round by my uncle's garden and they found a skeleton. They were so excited he didn't like to say he'd been digging them up for years and putting them in the dustbin.'

36

'Why the dustbin?'

'Well,' said Mrs Harrison, reasonably, 'they were in the way, weren't they? You'd do better to go and dig on the council tip. They're probably still there.'

Matthew saw that she was not going to provide much encouragement in this venture. To get away he pretended to notice Mum in the garden and retreated through the hedge. As a reward for his deceit he found that Mum really was waiting for him on the other side, with a shopping basket.

'Are you busy?' she asked in a voice that meant that she didn't think so, whether he did or not.

'I'm digging,' he said, 'my excavation.'

'That nonsense,' said Mum. 'That can wait. I want you to take this back to Charlie.' She gave him the bag and he looked inside. It contained the biscuit tin that the hare had come in, and two cabbages.

'Charlie's ploughing,' said Matthew.

'Then leave that at the door,' said Mum. 'You've got plenty of time to dig later. Anyway, I don't think Mrs Collinge meant you to go digging holes. She wants you to write something, I expect.'

'I will write,' said Matthew, taking the bag. 'But I'll dig as well. You won't tell her, will you? If I do find anything I'd like that to be a surprise.'

'That'll be a surprise, right enough,' said Mum. 'What's she going to put on your report this term? Matthew has dug some very nice holes? Ten out of ten for a big one?'

He took the bag and went onto the footpath, through the garden gate. It was very difficult to keep home affairs secret from school. When Mum had finished washing up after lunch she joined Mrs Collinge and Miss Cooper for a cup of tea and a cosy chat before afternoon lessons began. Matthew often suspected that some of the cosy chats were about him, so it was equally difficult to keep school secrets away from home. Roger Howlett was the school nuisance but if it hadn't been for Mum being the dinner lady, Matthew might be the school nuisance with Roger a close second.

As he walked down the path to the farm Charlie came bucketing up the field trailing his own snowstorm: a wheeling funnel of seagulls that rose and rolled behind the plough. Ahead of him Yew ran in tight circles, nose to the ground. When Matthew went by the dog ran after him, trying to leap into his arms.

When he was a puppy Charlie had carried him about tucked inside his jacket, and Yew, now four years old, still thought that this was a good way to travel although he was huge and heavy and looked like a torpedo with legs. Charlie leaned from his cab, shouting and whistling, but Yew ran round in front of Matthew and waylaid him by rising on his hind legs and putting his arms round Matthew's neck. He smiled his silly smile and leaned his head on Matthew's shoulder, sighing like a furnace. In the end Charlie had to stop the tractor and come back down the field to fetch him.

'Come down off of that, you great soft fool,' said Charlie, seizing Yew by the collar and tail and dragging him away. Yew sat down on Charlie's feet. He was a big man but he staggered slightly. 'You ought to be beat,' said Charlie, not very convincingly. He looked at his watch. 'Half past ten. Come and have a cup of tea.'

Charlie was a great timekeeper. He always had his midmorning break at exactly ten-thirty and if he happened to be at the top of the field when it was time to stop he had his tea at Matthew's house instead. At the moment they were marginally nearer the farm so they walked down the field.

'I was coming to see you,' said Matthew, holding up the bag. 'Mum sent this back, she's put some cabbages in.'

'Very nice,' said Charlie. 'I miss the garden, sometimes. Have to put a few vegetables in again, one of these days.'

Charlie had ploughed up his garden some years ago and

now his fields stretched right up to the kitchen door. He and Matthew walked out of the stubble and onto the door-step without pause. Yew went back to annoy the seagulls who were settling in the furrows, waiting for Charlie to return and serve the next course.

'Put that bag down and have a seat,' said Charlie, throwing his cap aside and lighting the stove that stood in the corner, next to the gas cylinder that fed it.

'Been gardening?' he asked, seeing Matthew's muddy hands.

'Sort of,' said Matthew. 'I've been digging a hole.' However much he wanted to keep the matter to himself he still found himself talking about it. Charlie only nodded.

'Why not?' he said.

Then he said 'Why?'

'You know that garden next to ours, belonging to the house that Dad bought?'

'Old Batty Blakely's?' said Charlie. 'Your Dad have got trouble there, I reckon.'

'Isn't the priory under it?'

'Priory's under my field, aren't it?' said Charlie, un-helpfully.

'I thought there might be a bit of it in our garden,' said Matthew. 'I thought I'd try and dig it up.'

'You must be short of a way to waste time,' said Charlie. He measured six spoonfuls of tea into the pot. 'I been turn-ing up that field for twenty-five years, and I never found nothing but flints. Sugar?'

'Yes, please. But you don't plough very deep, do you? I was going to dig right down.'

Charlie handed him thick, brown tea in a thin, pink cup, standing in a blue and white striped saucer. The saucer that matched the cup was on the floor with the remains of Yew's breakfast in it.

'I don't think depth have got much to do with it,' said Charlie. 'I just don't reckon there's anything to find, that's

39

all. The only bit I know of was what my old Dad turned up, and he was ploughing with the horses.'

'What did he find?' asked Matthew, swallowing hard. The tea was furry and seemed to stick, all the way down.

'You come in here and I'll show you,' said Charlie, leading the way into the living-room. Matthew followed. He often visited Charlie but this was the first time he had got further than the kitchen. Since old Mr Hemp died, Charlie lived in the kitchen, coming out of it only on Sundays, to dust.

The living-room was cold and green: green carpet, green chairs, and a green tablecloth. Green curtains hung at the windows, faded to the colour of cabbage stalks. Matthew stayed in the doorway, afraid to soil this green sanctuary with his boots.

'Here,' said Charlie. 'Take a look at this.' He beckoned Matthew to the fireplace which stood in the wall, opposite the door, as high as Charlie's shoulder and as sturdy as a little stone house.

'My old Dad, he made this himself,' said Charlie, patting the mantlepiece. Matthew came forward to look. The fireplace was built of grey stone blocks, roughly faced.

'Did he find all the stone in the field?' asked Matthew. Charlie was being rather off-hand about it, if so.

'No, he bought that,' said Charlie. 'This here's what he found.' In the middle of the course above the grate were three blocks with carving on them. Two were ribbed like the stones over the church porch but the middle one bore a figure, a little square bird with staring stone eyes and stout claws, gripping a crescent moon.

Matthew ran his hand over it.

'Is that an owl?'

'That's right,' said Charlie. 'The owl in the moon, we called that.'

'Where's the rest of it?'

'Where's the rest of what?'

'The rest of the priory,' said Matthew. 'If that's all that was left, what happened to the rest of it?'

'How should I know?' said Charlie. 'Maybe this weren't off the priory at all. That was found up at Myhill Street, that's all I know.'

'It must be very old.'

'Yes,' said Charlie. 'So don't tell no one or we'll be full up with people coming to see it.'

'If I dug up something like that, it would be from the priory, wouldn't it?'

'That's right,' said Charlie. 'You dig up owls.' He led the way back to the kitchen. 'Tea'll be getting cold.'

Yew was in the kitchen, standing on his hind legs with his elbows on the table, drinking out of Matthew's over-turned cup. He lowered his eyelids modestly as they came in but he didn't stop drinking.

'Have another cup,' said Charlie, giving Yew a shove that was supposed to knock him off the table, but only made him hiccough, resonantly.

'No, I won't, thanks,' said Matthew. 'I ought to get back and start digging.'

Charlie, engaged in pushing Yew to the floor, gave him an absent-minded wave as he went out.

Walking up the field he could see that something was happening at home. Figures moved about in the new garden and a ladder was placed against the wall of Kingston Villa. As he drew nearer, someone came out from behind the chimney stack and scrambled across the tiles. Matthew began to run. Behind the trees he could see one of the Angels' lorries, parked in the loke. Astride the roof sat Chris Angel, prising up ridge tiles and slinging them into the garden.

Mrs Harrison called over the fence 'I see your company have arrived.'

6. Angels on the Roof

As Matthew entered through the garden gate Mum leaned out of the kitchen window and jerked her thumb at him.

'Don't stand there unless you want a hole in your head. He's got as much sense of direction as a turnip.'

Matthew stepped aside. Some of the tiles had landed on the home side of the hedge. As he watched, one came down in the privet.

Matthew waved at Chris in case he should happen to be looking that way, and hurried up the garden.

'Where's Mr Angel?' he asked, in the kitchen.

'Banging about inside,' said Mum. 'I can hear him through the bedroom wall. There's another one with him, somewhere, and a little boy.'

'That's Clive,' said Matthew. 'Julie and Karen aren't here, then. I'll get on with my digging.' He wanted to be out there immediately, to follow the clue of the owl, before it began to seem ridiculous.

'You're not going out there until that fellow's come down off the roof,' said Mum. 'In any case, isn't it time you forgot about digging and thought about your history?'

'That is history,' said Matthew. 'And I've hardly begun to dig, yet.'

'If you don't want me to tell Mrs Collinge about it you'd better think of something you can tell her about yourself,' said Mum.

This was blackmail. Matthew put his boots behind the

kitchen door and went upstairs to his bedroom. It was strange how everyone found his school work more interesting than he did. He sat on the bed and looked out of the window. Down below, in the new garden, someone was standing in the excavation, drawing the outlines of it with his foot. Matthew lowered his head behind the aquarium where the stick-insects lived and peered through the privet stems. One of the stems moved stiffly away on wiry legs and left a space for him to look through.

The person in the garden was staring up at the roof. A pantile, caught on a current of air, volplaned into view and skimmed over his head. The person only stood there, his arms folded, like an early martyr who considered it beneath his dignity to duck. Matthew recognized him as the unidentified Angel who had emerged last of all from the green bungalow, on Saturday. He was fair haired while Chris was dark, but he looked enough like him to be his brother, flat faced and genial. Another tile went over his head, close enough to lift his hair as it passed.

'Do you have to stand just there, Paul?' said Chris's voice, from above.

'I like the excitement,' said Paul, placidly.

'I wish you'd go away,' said Chris, and the next tile came down with more than necessary force. It hit the earth in Matthew's excavation and a cloud of dust enveloped Paul's ankles.

'You did that on purpose,' said Paul, surprised but without resentment. He began to move, very casually, towards the hedge. Chris sent another tile after him, to make sure he kept moving. He disappeared behind the hedge and dodged through the gap into Matthew's garden. Matthew, still stooping out of sight behind the stick-insects, ran downstairs and into the kitchen.

Mum was washing clothes at the sink and watching Paul through the window. He was standing under the plum tree, making a variety of rude gestures towards the roof.

43

'Where are you going?' asked Mum, as Matthew tried to slip out of the door. 'You aren't going out into the garden.'

'He's out there,' said Matthew, pointing to Paul at the moment when he picked up a clod of earth and hurled it upwards and out of sight. 'He shouldn't be doing that in our garden.'

'No, I suppose not,' said Mum, too engrossed in the performance to pay attention.

If it had been Matthew out there, delivering missiles at the roof and using insulting behaviour, he would have been hauled in at once.

He said as much, since Mum obviously wasn't listening. 'Can I ask him in?' he added, more loudly.

'I reckon you'd better,' said Mum. 'I think I'll have a word with George when I next see him.' Another tile crashed through the branches of the plum tree. Paul was being driven into the cauliflowers, behind the garage. 'Go out the front way and catch him as he comes round.'

Matthew raced to the front door, already curtained and sealed against winter, drew the bolts and dragged it open just as Paul jumped backwards into the porch. Chris, pursuing him implacably, was now throwing tiles into the front garden.

'He shouldn't do that,' said Matthew, bolting the door.

'You don't have to lock up, he can't throw them in,' said Paul.

'I know that, but it's meant to be bolted,' said Matthew. 'He shouldn't throw tiles into our garden.'

'He wasn't trying to hit me.'

Matthew thought that Paul took too charitable a view of the situation.

'My Mum'll tell him to stop.'

'He's my brother,' said Paul, as if that gave Chris powers of life and death over him. 'He's all right.'

'He was all right to me,' said Matthew, doubtfully. 'I met him on Saturday when I took a note over to yours.'

'Oh yes. You ran away when you saw me coming,' said Paul.

'I didn't. I just had to go,' said Matthew. 'Anyway, Julie and Karen were there. I see enough of them at school.'

'My cousins,' said Paul. 'They're all right.' It appeared that Matthew was not allowed to criticize Paul's relatives. 'I can't hear anything. Let's go out again.'

'I'll just let my Mum know,' said Matthew, making for the kitchen. Paul stopped him.

'You don't have to ask her if you can go out, do you?'

'Of course not. I was just going to tell her he's finished. She wanted to know.' Paul was certainly older than he, but not so much older that he could assume that Matthew was a little boy. To preserve his reputation Matthew had to go back to the front door and draw all the bolts again so that they could get out without Mum noticing.

Matthew looked up at the roof as they left the shelter of the porch. Chris had not finished but he had his back to them and the sound of distant smashing told him that the tiles were landing in the back garden again. The roof had a threadbare look with the laths exposed.

'It's in a terrible mess, that place,' said Paul. 'Dad said he'd never seen anything like it. Why did your Dad buy it?'

'We need more room,' said Matthew. 'We've only got two bedrooms.'

'Three,' said Paul.

'Two.'

'There's three next door.'

'One of ours is a bathroom now,' said Matthew. Paul looked like being another Darren when it came to arguments. 'I should know. When my Gran comes to stay I have to sleep on the settee. And Mum thought we might do a bit of bed and breakfast, in the summer.'

'My Auntie Molly does that, over at Tokesby,' said Paul. 'But she's got a big house and it's near the sea. You wouldn't get anyone to stay here, would you?'

It seemed that Paul could say what he liked.

'Why not?' said Matthew. 'People ask, sometimes. We had a Mr and Mrs Myhill here, last summer, from America. They were looking for ancestors, but they couldn't find any. They wanted somewhere to stay the night but we had to send them to "The Wherry", in Polthorpe.'

'What made them think they'd find ancestors here?' asked Paul, looking up and down the flinty loke. 'There's nothing here.'

'That was the name,' said Matthew. 'This bit's called Myhill Street.'

'Ship Loke,' said Paul.

'Ship Loke's in Myhill Street.'

'We call it Mile Street,' said Paul.

'So do we,' said Matthew. 'But they didn't. They called it My-hill Street. They gave me their address, so I could send them a Christmas card. It was a town called Keswick – but they called it Kes-wick.'

'I bet they didn't find any ancestors,' said Paul. He strolled into the garden of Kingston Villa. Mr Angel had taken the gate off its hinges and reversed his lorry up the front path.

'Mum showed them the phone book,' said Matthew. 'There are dozens of Myhills in that. I showed them the priory.'

'A priory?' said Paul. 'Where is it? I can't see any priory.'

'You're standing on it,' said Matthew. 'That's all under-ground.' Before he could stop himself, he added, 'I'm going to dig that up.'

Paul started to look amused and then tapped his chin and became thoughtful, as though he had pressed a button to change his expression.

'What makes you think you'll find anything?' he asked.

'Your brother Chris did,' said Matthew. 'That was his idea.'

'If Chris thinks there's something here, there must be,' said Paul, very gravely.

'I'm not telling anyone until I've found something,' said Matthew, mentally crossing out all the people he had told already. 'Don't say anything to Julie and Karen, I want to keep it a secret from Mrs Collinge.'

'Who's she?' asked Paul. He was looking at the ground with a speculative eye, considering what might be under it.

'Our teacher,' said Matthew. 'I don't reckon she'd think that was a very good idea, not for school work, I mean, so I'm going to keep quiet until I've dug something up.'

'We could tell Chris,' said Paul, 'as that was his idea in the first place. He's reading History at university, next year. He might be able to help – with advice I mean. He wouldn't dig.'

Matthew liked the way that Paul said 'we'. He had an ally at last.

'Of course, archaeologists don't dig in winter,' said Paul, lowering his hopes again. 'They have to pack up in the autumn and wait for summer. They go on telly in winter.'

'I can't wait,' said Matthew. 'I've only got until January, I reckon. Dad's going to start digging it properly, after that. If I don't find anything by Christmas, I'll have to pack that in. That's been a dry autumn; it's easy to dig at the moment.'

'Yeeeeees,' said Paul, making the word last while he thought of an argument. 'We might have a downpour any day. It would be like digging in a Christmas pudding. Where's your excavation?'

'Over there,' said Matthew, pointing.

'Not that funny little hole I was standing in? Really? You haven't got very far, have you?'

'I only started last night,' said Matthew. 'When I came down this morning, Mum sent me out for something, and when I came back Chris was chucking tiles about. I had to go in.'

'Well, he's stopped now,' said Paul, glancing up at the

roof. Chris had gone, leaving the ladder and a bald patch among the tiles. 'It must be time for our tea break.'

He walked up to the kitchen window of Kingston Villa and looked through the dirty glass, making a little peaked roof with his hands.

'Nobody there.' He looked frantic. 'Where've they gone? Clive's not there either.'

Matthew was disturbed to see Paul so worried by so little. 'I expect they're round at ours. Perhaps your Dad wanted to boil a kettle, or something.'

'Yes, that's probably it,' said Paul, looking relieved. 'Let's go and see.' He burrowed through the gap in the hedge, leaving Matthew to follow. Matthew thought that it should be Paul following him, since Paul was the visitor, especially when Paul opened the kitchen door and walked in, without knocking. Matthew looked over his shoulder and saw the kitchen full of people. Dad had dropped in on his way back from a breakdown and he was sitting at the table drinking tea with Mum, Mr Angel, and Chris.

'What's all this, then?' said Mr Angel as Paul came in. 'I thought you were meant to be helping.'

'When did you go out?' said Mum, to Matthew.

'Oh,' said Paul. 'I was just going up the ladder when I saw some interesting fungus in the garden. Had to go and look.'

'He's cursed with perfect eyesight,' said his father.

Mum poured two more cups of tea and pushed the biscuit tin towards them.

'When did you go out?' she said, fixing Matthew with an angry eye.

Chris didn't speak. He was looking under the table and out into the hall. Suddenly he roared, 'Come here!' and grimy Clive ran in. He didn't stop, but hurtled on, into the garden. As he passed the table his arm flicked out, quick as a toad's tongue and the last of the biscuits disappeared with him.

48

'He don't miss a trick, do he?' said Mr Angel, as though Clive were a performing seal. 'Come on, boys. Back to work.'

The Angels all left together and a few minutes later thumping broke out again, next door.

'Now, when did you go out?' demanded Mum, ready for battle.

'Paul wanted to go out,' said Matthew.

'Don't blame him.'

'We did wait till Chris had stopped – stopped throwing them at Paul, I mean,' said Matthew. 'Is that all the Angels?'

'I don't know, I've lost count,' said Mum. 'Lively, aren't they?'

'Don't stop counting yet,' said Dad. 'George thought John might be along after lunch, and he usually brings his little girls with him, to play with Clive. George don't like to leave him running about on his own.'

'Why bring him then?' said Mum, clearing the table. 'He shouldn't be running about on a building site at his age.'

Dad looked sidelong at Matthew and said quietly, 'You know . . .'

'Oh, yes,' said Mum, also glancing his way to see if he were listening. Matthew tried to make out if this shorthand had anything to do with him; then he realized what Dad had said.

'Julie and Karen coming here?' he shouted. If they arrived and found him digging he would never make any progress. They would go to extraordinary lengths to avoid being ignored. He sometimes thought that Julie would willingly hang herself if it would draw an audience. He ran to the toolshed to fetch the spade, remembered that it was already out there, doubled back and dived through the hedge. All the Angels were indoors but as soon as he began to dig Paul came out.

'You'll never get through all that grass,' he said.

'I've cut enough to be getting on with,' said Matthew. 'Dad will do the rest with a scythe, but he won't let me use it.'

'I can handle a scythe. Hang on. I'll just ask your Dad,' said Paul, bounding through the hedge.

He was back, very quickly, with the scythe that was kept, not in the toolshed, but out of Matthew's reach in the rafters of the garage. Dad was afraid that Matthew would cut off his feet with it but presumably he thought that Paul's feet were his own affair.

Matthew wished that he had refused Paul as well, all the same.

Paul began his operations under the oak tree, where the grass was green and silky, untarnished by the weather. Matthew continued to dig. After a while, Clive wandered out with plaster in his hair.

'I dig,' he said, succinctly, and flung himself down on his knees, tearing at the earth with his hands.

'He doesn't look quite human, does he?' said aul, leaning on the scythe and watching his brother worrying at the turf. 'When he gets a bit older we'll tie a string round his leg and send him down holes after rabbits.'

7. The Antiquary

By the time Matthew had finished his lunch there was another yellow lorry in the loke. He ran round to the front garden and was just in time to see Mr John Angel lifting Karen from the driver's cab. Julie was standing at the gate. Mr John went straight into the house, leaving the girls in the loke, staring at Matthew.

'We're going into your garden,' said Karen. 'We can go into your garden when we like. Daddy said.'

'If you behave yourself,' said Matthew. He was holding the spade. It would be so simple to lift it high in the air and bring it down on Karen's head.

'We can go in anyway. When we like. You can't stop us,' said Julie, squeezing past the lorry in the gateway. Karen skipped after her and Matthew stood and watched them over the hedge.

'You're not Head Boy here,' said Julie. Clive looked out of the front door, pale with dust.

'What are you going to do? Smash all the windows?' said Matthew.

Clive blinked at him. 'I dig,' he said with a dismissive wave of the hand, and strode unsteadily after his cousins, round the corner of the house. Matthew returned to his own back garden and squinted through the privet. In spite of his threat Clive was not digging. The new garden was deserted, although Matthew could hear shrill cries from inside Kingston Villa. He went across to the excavation and plunged the spade into the earth. As it landed he heard the blade strike metal and when he pulled it out, along with a generous helping of earth, he saw something lumpy in the hole: an iron hand with rusty claws.

He went down on his knees, and dug at his discovery, holding the spade just above the blade, like a paddle. The lumpy thing did not come out of the hole, it was too deeply embedded, but the earth crumbled away round it. He looked to see if Paul was anywhere near, to help him, but Paul had been conscripted after lunch and the scythe lay idle against the oak tree.

He pulled the sleeves of his sweater over his hands and took hold of the object. It resisted his tugging and the iron bit into his sleeves, laddering them for a considerable distance.

'You'll get ever so wrong for that,' said a pleased voice beside him. Karen was standing in the hole.

'That's only an old one. Go away. Go indoors,' said Matthew, looking at his sleeves.

'She doesn't have to if you say so,' said Julie, stepping into the hole beside her sister.

'I've brought my dolly,' said Karen, holding it out. It was a pale, rubbery creature, heavily tattooed all over with a blue ball point pen.

'You take your dolly away or I'll bury it, and you too,' said Matthew, sitting back on his heels. 'Get out of my excavation.' The object was beginning to work free of the earth. It was certainly nothing that Sir Oliver had ever set eyes on. It looked like a piece of roofing iron and he re-called that the Blakelys had buried their sheds just about here. Still, it was going to save him some hard labour when he finally got it out, for there was a large hollow under-neath.

'I'm going to tell my Daddy what you said,' remarked Julie. 'And I'm going to tell Mrs Collinge.' She never used any particular tone with her threats. She might have been reciting a boring poem.

'Go and tell a tree,' said Matthew. He gave a final heave and rolled over as the iron jerked out of the earth. The trench where it had been lying was so full of leggy, leathery insects that Julie and Karen leaped out of the hole and cantered back to the house, leaving Matthew in possession. There was something else in the hole: a green teaspoon with N.C.C. stamped on the handle. He hoped for a moment that it was an antique, religious sort of spoon, such as medieval monks might have used, and that N.C.C. stood for something holy, but he knew that it was more likely to mean that the spoon was the property of the Norfolk County Council and not at all ancient, especially as it said Made in Sheffield on the back.

That wasn't going to earn it a place in the British Museum or even the school museum.

Using the new trench as a starting place he began to dig again where the earth was damp and soft. The soil was full of whiskery roots that had no plants growing from them, a secret, underground network that nourished nothing. He dug with one eye to the ground and one on Kingston Villa, ready to repel any Angels that might come out. At one point he saw Julie in the kitchen, adding eyelashes and curly hair to the face that he had drawn on the window, but she remained indoors.

The spade struck iron again. Little clods of earth fell away from the root fronds and he saw another strip of roof. There was no need to treat it gently this time, as he knew in advance that it wasn't historic. He wedged the spade under the iron and pressed down. The iron began to rise out of the ground with a tearing sound, lifting a long mat of grass with it.

'That could be the end of a very nice spade,' said Chris Angel, crossing the garden. He had Paul with him and at their heels shambled Clive, shoulders up, head down, a little black shadow.

'I dig,' said Clive, laying hands on the spade. Matthew didn't care to boot him off with his brothers watching but Chris picked him up and put him down again, a little way off.

'What have you found?' said Paul. 'An air raid shelter?'

Matthew hadn't thought of this. It was a long time since the end of the war: surely air raid shelters were getting historic by now?

'Wrong shape for an air raid shelter,' said Chris, holding Clive at bay with his foot. Matthew's short dream faded.

'That must be the Blakelys' garden shed,' he explained. 'Mr Blakely who used to own this house, he buried three sheds and a greenhouse. I've got to get past them before I find anything. Well, I did find this.' He held out the green teaspoon. 'I think it's a modern one.'

Chris was very serious about the spoon. He examined it carefully.

'A buried artifact,' he said, turning it over and over. 'You ought to put it back. Someone may come and dig here when we're dead and gone. Think how excited they'll be to find this prehistoric cutlery.'

'That's not prehistoric,' said Matthew.

'It will be in three thousand years,' said Chris. 'In three thousand years those sheds you mentioned – they'll be prehistoric. At least, they will be if you don't dig them up first.'

'We'll never be prehistoric,' said Matthew. 'I know what that means. What about films and tape-recordings and books? Dinosaurs are only prehistoric because they couldn't write.'

Chris nodded, but he had to disagree, as people so often did with Matthew.

'Books and tape-recordings will survive if we look after them, but just think, when they've all perished in the

54

nuclear holocaust your sheds will still be here, buried deep. And your teaspoon.'

'What holocaust?' said Matthew, making sure that he said it right first time.

'Armageddon – the great devastation,' said Chris, tapping his nose with the teaspoon.

'What's that?'

Chris lost patience.

'Oh Jesus,' he said, and flung the teaspoon into the hole. Clive dived in after it.

'Don't be hard on him,' said Paul, with a pitying look in Matthew's direction. 'You see,' he said earnestly, to Matthew, 'all that stuff you find in museums was what people threw out as rubbish in the old days. They didn't know that archaeologists were going to come along thousands of years later and dig it all up again. The Martians might come and dig up those sheds. That teaspoon might end up in a Martian museum.'

'You know what a Martian is, don't you?' said Chris.

'He hasn't had your advantages,' said Paul. 'He hasn't been taught history by Frederick Kenworthy Bagnall, M.A. That is an advantage, isn't it?'

'Is his name Kenworthy?' said Matthew. 'That just says F. K. Bagnall on his brief-case.'

'Do you know him, then?' asked Chris. 'We're great friends, sometimes.'

'He lives in that bungalow,' said Matthew, pointing over the wall.

Paul leaped up. 'Let's go and see him,' he said at once.

'You can't. They've gone away for a couple of days,' said Matthew. 'I've got to feed their cats tonight. That's a good thing you reminded me.'

'You'd better not let him know what you're doing,' said Chris. 'He can't bear amateurs digging things up. Damned antiquarians, he calls them.'

'What's an antiquarian?'

'Oh Jeeeee – dear, dear, dear,' said Chris. 'Some people have fairies at the bottom of the garden. You've got Frederick M.A. at the bottom of yours and you don't know what an antiquarian is?'

'I only talk to him on Saturdays,' said Matthew.

'How quaint,' said Chris. 'What do you do the rest of the week, throw things?'

'What's an antiquarian?'

'In the nineteenth century,' said Chris, 'a lot of tiresome old gentlemen with nothing better to do went round digging for history, just like you. They caused terrible damage to historic sites because they didn't understand what they found. They only kept things if they liked the look of them. They called themselves antiquaries but today they'd be called vandals and magistrates would be extremely sharp with them.'

Matthew felt great shame. He was an antiquary if ever there was one.

'That was your idea,' he said.

'Yes, but I didn't know you lived next door to Frederick when I suggested it,' said Chris. 'Worse things happened earlier than that, when people dug for treasure and thought about its value only in terms of money. Look what happened to the three crowns of East Anglia.'

'What three crowns?'

'My God, he's hopeless,' said Chris to Paul, and sat down on the edge of the excavation. It looked like being a long lecture so Paul and Matthew sat down too. Clive went on rooting about in the background.

Chris wore a particularly joyless expression. He seemed to have caught something besides history from Mr Bagnall. Like him, it was impossible to tell whether he was joking, if indeed he ever was.

'Once upon a time,' said Chris.

'There were three bears,' said Paul. Without looking at him, Chris gave him a frightful clout on the head. Paul rolled into the excavation but he seemed accustomed to such treatment and righted himself without complaint.

'There were three crowns buried in East Anglia to protect the kingdom from invasion. The kingdom of East Anglia, that is. In those days they weren't so bothered about the rest of England.'

'They're not so bothered now,' said Paul. 'Are we? Home rule for Norfolk. Let's start an East Anglian Liberation Front.'

'Shut up,' said Chris, drawing back his elbow, preliminary to another assault. Paul eased himself along the lip of the hole. 'Those crowns were no joke. People really believed they were there. In fact, they probably were there. In the seventeenth century they dug up an ancient silver crown at Rendlesham, and I hardly like to tell you what happened to that. It's not fit for young ears.'

'They melted it down.'

'You'd better not melt down your teaspoon,' said Paul. 'But there's one crown left, isn't there, Chris? That's why we weren't invaded during the war.'

'Fact,' said Chris. Matthew looked from one to the other. They regarded him with Bagnall-like faces.

'What about William the Conqueror?' said Matthew.

'Tea time,' said Chris, although it was only three o'clock, and walked away with his brothers in meek attendance, leaving Matthew to decide whether he was offended or laughing. He was beginning to notice that if he got things wrong people despised him, and if he got them right they thought he was funny. Life was full of jokes that he failed to appreciate. It was a great conspiracy.

When it really was tea time the Angels were still working in Kingston Villa and it was growing dark before they came out and climbed into their several lorries. Matthew risked seeing them off.

'Will you be here tomorrow?' he asked Paul who was riding home on the back of the lorry, among the ladders.

'We won't. It's Tokesby again, tomorrow,' said Paul. 'Uncle John will be, though.'

'And Julie and Karen?'

'No, they're going out for the day with Clive,' said Paul. 'We'll be back on Saturday.'

A thought struck him.

'By the way, why do you only talk to Frederick M.A. on Saturdays?'

'I don't see him the rest of the week,' said Matthew. 'On Saturdays I deliver his eggs.'

'I didn't know he laid eggs,' said Paul. 'There's a tale to tell the lads. Bye bye. Have a nice dig.' He knocked on the rear window of the cab to let his father know he was ready, and the lorries rolled away.

Matthew went home to collect the key that Mrs Bagnall had given him.

The proper way to reach the Bagnalls' bungalow was to go out of the front gate, down Ship Loke, into the Hoxenham Road and round to the front gate of their garden. Matthew went through the new garden and over the wall at the corner, behind the oak tree. Charlie, still ploughing, had switched on his headlights and the beams swept up and down the field, dealing Matthew a blinding blow in the eye as the tractor turned at the bottom of the slope. For some reason the sight of Charlie's headlights gave him a cold itch at the back of the neck, but he couldn't remember why.

He walked across the Bagnalls' garden, under the apple trees, dark against a darkening sky, and felt his way to the door by following the little pink bead of light that shone behind the bell push. On the doorstep he felt a soft billowing about his feet and when he opened the door and switched on the light, the cats streamed into the kitchen, purring melodiously.

There was a little wicket gate cut for them at the base of the door, but they preferred to wait on the step for Mrs Bagnall when she came home from school.

They rose on their hind legs and fell against the furniture, apparently weak with hunger. Mr Bagnall said that cats were natural twisters and liked to wave the meat plate over their heads to make them sing louder. Matthew took the plate from the fridge and tried the same experiment. The purring rose to a contralto trill. All six cats were there, with their curious names: Genghis Khan, Jones the Bookrest, Furbelow, Supercat, Tokyo Rose, who was foreign, and Minnie, who was expecting kittens. Matthew suspected more jokes but was afraid to ask.

He put the plate on the floor and it was engulfed in fur. He poured fresh milk and water into the special pussy bowls labelled 'Milk' and 'Water', turned off the light and shut the door on the diners.

As he turned the key he heard a faint sound in the darkness, above the distant churning of the tractor. He stood still, ears expanding, and then ran like hell for the wall. He had just remembered what Charlie's headlights reminded him of.

Just a silly story, according to Mum.

Sir Oliver.

8. The Deputy

Matthew rode out on Wednesday morning under low, fast-moving clouds. The wind swept him down the Hoxenham Road on a tide of swirling leaves, a brown, autumn river that ran between green banks where yarrow, white campions and dandelions were still in flower. He coasted past the summer flowers and the winter trees until he reached the dell where the sycamores, standing low in the damp soil, were as green as September, and the gas stoves were half hidden from sight.

He paused by the dell and stared down into the hollow; and remembered what Chris had said about today's rubbish being tomorrow's history. Every year the falling leaves lay a little further up the sides of the stoves. One day they would be covered. One day the leaves would rise to the top of the dell and the ground would be level again, with the gas stoves buried, deep down.

In thousands of years, spaceships might land on the recreation ground. Archaeologists with four arms would trundle out, carrying complicated implements with which to excavate the gas stoves, and wondering about the small, primitive people who had set them up and worshipped them. It was certain that the people who had dumped them there in the first place had never thought that they would become an ancient monument.

Looking over his shoulder Matthew saw the morning milk-float approaching him from behind, and this made him hurry on again. He had no watch and might be late. Usually he arrived just in time but now that he was Head Boy he ought to be there earlier than anyone else, in case a fight broke out or one of the infants shut her finger in the gate.

Just before he reached the school there was a slight bend in the road so that he approached unseen. That way he knew what was going on before anyone noticed him, so when he reached the gates and found Karen Angel and Roger Howlett shoving up against them, he knew something of what had happened before he began asking questions.

'Why did you hit her?' he asked, herding them into the playground.

'I never,' said Roger.

Karen rolled up her sleeve. 'He did. He hit me here.' There was a small, black bruise.

'You got that on Monday,' said Matthew. 'Hitting Clive. You missed and hit the wheelbarrow instead. My Mum had to dab that for you.'

Julie came out from behind the cycle shed.

'He did hit her. He hit me too, but I got away,' said Julie.

'He shouldn't have hit my poorly bruise,' said Karen. 'I'm telling of him to Miss Cooper.'

Matthew felt that anyone who hit the Angel sisters was only obeying the laws of nature, but it wasn't allowed and had to be stopped.

'You're not telling anyone,' he said. 'Miss Cooper's got enough to do. What did you hit her for, anyway?' he asked Roger, when Julie and Karen had retired to the cloakroom to whip up a posse.

'Julie said I'd get worms from eating orange peel and I gave her a shove and Karen bit me so I shoved her too,' said Roger, plaintively. 'I shoved her with my foot.'

'Biting's worse than hitting,' said Matthew, wondering what he ought to do about it. 'Let's have a look.' Roger exhibited his thumb with two faint dents in it.

'I don't call that much,' said Matthew. 'Besides, Karen hasn't got any bottom teeth. That's only half a bite, and she's smaller than you.' He went after Julie and Karen. 'If you don't say anything about being hit, Roger won't say anything about the biting.'

'Just because you're Head Boy,' said Julie, but she walked away without arguing.

It was hard to have to see them at home as well as in school, but at least in school he had only to bother with Julie. Karen was in the infant class on the other side of the partition. He could hear her squealing but it was only one squeal among fourteen others. There were eighteen juniors and that was the whole school: thirty-three of them, or thirty-eight if you counted Mrs Collinge and Miss Cooper, Mum and Mrs Sadler at lunch-time, and Roger Howlett's granny who was the caretaker.

Roger lolled on Mrs Collinge's desk while Matthew laid out the registers, looked up the number of today's hymn and opened the book on the piano.

'Can you get worms from eating orange peel?' he asked.

'You should have thought of that before you hit her,' said Matthew. 'I don't expect so, she just likes frightening people. She told me once that grass grows through your lungs if you swallow it.' He heard Mrs Collinge's car pull up on the grit by the gates. 'Come on, you shouldn't be in here yet. Go and line up with the others.'

Roger left the room and immediately Matthew heard another fight start up outside because Roger had put himself at the head of the line and there was someone else there already. He decided that it was Mrs Collinge s turn to deal with this one, and went to open the partition between the two rooms so that both classes could join in assembly. After it was finished he would have to close it again. Old Mrs Howlett was in the infants' room, wiping the tables with a damp rag.

'That Roger,' was all she said. 'I'm off home now. Tell

Mrs Collinge there's paint down the sink again and not to use the tap. I'll see to that this evening.'

'But that was all right on Friday,' said Matthew.

'Miss Cooper were in over half term, doing charts,' said Mrs Howlett. 'Paint everywhere. She's worse than you children.'

Matthew thought that Mrs Howlett should not say such things to him. Miss Cooper was certainly untidy; he and Darren often spent whole playtimes helping her find things, but she was very nice to him, personally. He sometimes wished that she and Mrs Collinge would change places. He heard Mrs Collinge coming into the junior room just then, and sprang to meet her, wearing a ready-made willing and eager look.

Mrs Collinge gave him what was meant to be a friendly smile but which made him feel as if he too needed wiping down with a damp rag.

'Good morning, Matthew,' she said, handing him some rolls of paper. 'Any messages? Will you put these up on the wall for me?'

'Mrs Howlett says the sink is blocked and not to use it,' said Matthew. 'Powder paint, again.' He did not mention Miss Cooper. Possibly Mrs Collinge had the same effect upon Miss Cooper as she had upon Matthew. He took the rolls of paper and opened them on the table with a book at each corner so that they wouldn't curl up. They were history posters with pictures of bygone people standing in front of their historic houses: a Stone Age family grovelling in a cave, a group of hooked-nosed Romans posing in front of their villa, and three scruffy Saxons scrabbling about in the earth round a thatched hut.

Mr Stone Age looked remarkably like Chris Angel, with the same large jaws, flat nose and sloping forehead. Baby Stone Age could easily have been Clive, smudgy and matted, searching for grubs under a stone. Mrs Stone Age looked like anybody's Mum, only wider. Matthew wondered for a moment what Mrs Angel looked like. He hadn't met her yet.

There were ten posters and Matthew found an acquaintance in most of them. Mr Saxon wore drooping moustaches like Roger's father's. Mrs Tudor Person had Mrs Collinge's habit of spying through her eye-lashes. Mr Middle Ages, with dog and long bow, was Charlie Hemp out after rabbits with Yew and a shotgun.

As he pinned them up he thought that perhaps the posters were meant to show that history was about ordinary people, who had lived lives as ordinary as his. This didn't make it any more attractive. He always saw the word 'history' with a red line drawn under it to show that it was finished, just as one day there would be a red line under him and he would be history too.

By now it was nine o'clock so he went to the door and called the line in. Mrs Collinge had made them wait outside for an extra five minutes, without talking, because of the fight.

'That's your fault,' said Peter Catchpole, who shared his table. 'We were waiting for you to come and stop us.'

'Why didn't you stop on your own?' said Matthew.

'That's your job,' said Peter, and made a quiet but disgusting noise that Matthew had never quite managed to master.

When morning break was over, Matthew collected all the bottles, put them in the crate, and stood them outside the kitchen door for the milkman to collect, tomorrow. While he was out he went round to the back of the building and looked across the fields to Myhill Street, to see if Mum was on her way yet. He searched the distance carefully and saw her at last, crossing Fen Street, a tiny red and white dot, which meant that she was wearing her new raincoat over the top of her overall. When he went inside again Mrs Collinge had arranged the class in a crescent, facing the

64

row of posters. Matthew took a chair at the end of the line, and sat down.

'May I have your work, Matthew?' said Mrs Collinge, extending her hand to receive it.

'Work?' said Matthew, sending his mind into reverse gear, to see if he could remember what she was talking about.

'Your holiday work,' said Mrs Collinge. 'Where is it?'

'I thought you asked us to think,' he said. The memory of Friday afternoon came back to him. 'You did ask us to think.'

There was a subdued laugh, all along the line, at the idea of Matthew thinking. When it reached Julie it became a papery cackle.

'That's enough of that,' said Mrs Collinge. 'I did ask you to think. I also asked you to write. I suppose you only remembered the bit you liked the sound of. I can't prove you haven't done it, can I?'

'Why try?' thought Matthew. Aloud he said 'Shall I write something now?'

'No,' said Mrs Collinge. 'If you do that you'll miss the next part. I want to be sure that you hear what I say, this time.' She walked away from him and swung round to face the class. 'When was this school built?'

Matthew looked along the row of faces, all wrinkled up with terrible effort, before he raised his hand. Mrs Collinge looked at him with some surprise.

'Eighteen sixty-nine,' said Matthew.

'Very good.'

'That's not fair,' said Peter. 'That's written over the front door.'

'Exactly,' said Mrs Collinge. 'So why didn't you know? You see, even the school is more than a hundred years old. That's history, isn't it? Now, the church is even older; more than six hundred years old. Who built it?'

Matthew looked down the line. The faces were wrinkling

up again. Peter Catchpole was gasping and hitting his forehead with the heel of his hand to show how hard he was thinking. Matthew didn't even consider the question. It had never occurred to him that anyone had built the church. It was just there, as it always had been. Perhaps Sir Oliver had built it. He raised his hand.

'Matthew?'

'Did Sir Oliver build it?' A look of pale despair clouded Mrs Collinge's face, like sea fog rolling across a field.

'We're talking about historical fact, not fairy tales,' she said.

'Sir Oliver's a ghost, Miss, not a fairy,' said Anne Lilley. Roger waved his arms about, making ghost noises but sounding like a distressed cow. Julie began to shriek at him. Matthew watched the class getting out of hand and knew that Mrs Collinge would blame him, privately, because he had been the first to mention Sir Oliver. Mrs Collinge couldn't know much about him because she came in from North Walsham every day by car. Pallingham people didn't talk about him, perhaps because he was so dull and they were ashamed of him.

'Sir Robert Coningbrook built the church in thirteen twenty-five,' said Mrs Collinge.

'All by himself with his bare hands?' said Peter Catchpole.

'Go and stand over there,' said Mrs Collinge, pointing to an obscure corner, and Peter took himself off making debonair faces because he had his back to her.

Sir Robert Coningbrook lay on the remains of a handsome stone monument, up by the altar in the church, with a self-satisfied smile on his face although his nose had worn down to the level of his moustache and time had whittled away his ankles. No wonder he looked so pleased with himself if he really had built the church, bare handed or not.

Mrs Collinge was still talking. Matthew drifted away. The

new police station at Polthorpe had a stone plaque in the porch with 1973 carved on it, and in the corner, two little initials, G.A., to show that the police station had been built by Geo. Angel. Builder and decorator. Maybe, in another hundred years another teacher would be standing here, asking who had put up the police station, and when the four-armed archaeologists came to dig it up, they might take Mr Angel's piece of stone and put it in a Martian museum, beside the long, helmeted skeleton of Sergeant Harvey, labelled 'Twentieth Century Policeman – Earth'.

He was brought back to the present by the sound of the kitchen door opening and closing. It was Mum, arriving to put the lunch in the oven.

'Now do you see what I mean?' Mrs Collinge was saying, and Matthew was glad she was not looking in his direction because he had not heard a word. 'You've got until the end of November.'

'When do we start?' said Roger.

'Today, if you like. I'll give out the paper after lunch. To make it easier, we shall all be visiting the museums in Norwich on the nineteenth.'

'That's my birthday on the nineteenth,' said Anne Lilley.

Matthew leaned across her lap and whispered to Roger, 'What do we have to finish at the end of November?'

'The charts,' said Roger.

'Get your fat elbow off my leg,' said Anne.

'What charts?'

'The history charts, like what we started over half term,' said Roger.

'All except you,' said Anne, with quiet malice, pushing Matthew out of the way.

9. Sheep

'How did you get on today?' asked Mum.

'I got a puncture on the way home,' said Matthew. This happened about once a month, so it was scarcely news.

'I meant at school. How do you like being Head Boy?'

'That's all right,' said Matthew. 'People do poke at you, though, to see what you'll do.'

'So long as you don't poke back,' said Mum. 'What did Mrs Collinge say about your history?'

'Not much,' said Matthew, unsure of what Mrs Collinge might have told Mum herself. 'We're still finding out about our houses and any old things in them. Do you know anything about our house?'

'That's too small,' said Mum. 'That's all I know. You'd better ask George. If he doesn't know now he soon will.'

Matthew reflected that people were not, after all, interested in his school work. They were only interested in him doing it.

'I'll just go and have a look round,' he said. 'Before that gets too dark,' and he went out. Mum thought he meant to go and look at Kingston Villa but instead he went down to the excavation. It was now a deep pit and piled to one side were all the pieces of Mr Blakely's shed that he had dug up. Whatever Chris thought about their archaeological value, they had to be moved before he could get any further. The only alternative was to dig another hole and that entailed moving sideways and not down.

Dad said that he was very pleased to see all the rubbish coming up and why didn't Matthew find the greenhouse as well, but he still thought he was wasting his time. He hadn't dared to fetch the spade while Mum thought he was looking at the house, but there was an old coal shovel behind the lean-to and he fetched that. After a week of damp November winds the ground was softening, but digging with the coal shovel was as efficient as digging with his teeth. He stood on the blade and rocked it into the ground. Something came up with the first attempt: it shone whitely in the dull light.

It was a bone.

Matthew dropped the shovel, picked up the bone and examined it closely. For a silly, happy second he thought it might be a monkish relic, a holy shoulder blade, perhaps, but strict regard for truth forced him to admit that it looked more like the kind of bone that came out of the joint on Sundays. It was probably the remains of a Blakely lunch.

'What are you doing?' called Mum, from the kitchen. As he was behind the hedge she couldn't see him and he hoped that it would be a long while yet before the hedge was removed.

'I'm just looking at the house,' he called back, slipping the bone under the iron roofing. To dilute the lie he went up to Kingston Villa and looked at it, hard.

'Everybody out,' said Mrs Collinge after lunch, on Friday. 'No excuses, please. You can do that later, Julie. I don't want anyone indoors while this fine weather lasts; it may rain tomorrow and you'll get no outdoor breaks at all. You too, Matthew.'

Matthew was hanging about by the big table, hoping for another look at the flint axe head that Peter Catchpole's grandfather had ploughed up on the day that Peter's father was born. Altogether the Catchpoles had found five of them, and they were usually sent to a museum in Norwich, but Mr Catchpole reckoned that this one was special so he kept it, and Peter was allowed to show it off, sometimes. He had loaned it, temporarily, to the school museum.

'My Grandad's got six fingers on his left hand,' said Peter, adding glamour to the axe head.

Mrs Collinge said that such things were left behind by people who had walked across to Norfolk from Germany, in the days when the North Sea lay far off, beyond the Dogger Bank. She showed them a map on which Great Britain was no more than a snout on the face of Europe, a smooth lump of land before the sea sank its teeth into it.

'Outside, Matthew,' said Mrs Collinge. 'Fresh air.' He also knew that she wanted a quiet cup of tea with Mum and Miss Cooper, if Miss Cooper had finished looking for her cigarettes under a heap of paint palettes, so he left the room and joined the others in the playground. Mrs Sadler, who kept an eye on them at lunch-time, was surrounded by the girls in his own class. The little ones were engaged in one of their huge games that took up the whole playground. Most of them were huddled at one end, by the gate. At the other end stood Mark Catchpole, the organizer and Peter's little brother.

'Do you want to be in our game?' asked Mark, generously.

'What is it?' said Matthew. He didn't think he ought to be playing with the little ones. Darren never did.

'Sheep and Shepherd,' said Mark. 'I'm the shepherd.'

'I'll just watch,' said Matthew, standing well back. All the infants' games ended with an enormous rush and minor injuries. Someone ought to watch them and he got ready to pick up casualties. Mark arranged himself in playing position. He yelled 'Sheep! Sheep! Come home at once.'

'We're afraid,' roared the sheep, milling round the gate.

'What of?'

'The wolf!'

'He's gone to Devonshire for a hundred years and he won't be back till December,' said the shifty shepherd.

The wolf had not gone to Devonshire. He was Trevor Lilley and he was hiding behind the lavatories. When the trustful sheep surged up the playground he jumped out of his covert and picked them off as they went past. Matthew ran to rescue a fallen sheep that looked as if it might cry, and noticed the usual argument breaking out among the rest of the flock.

'I'm shepherd now,' said Karen Angel. 'I wasn't caught.'

'Yes you were. I'm still shepherd,' said Mark. 'The wolf touched you.'

'That didn't.'

'That did. That touched your hair.'

'That did not.'

'I never touched her hair,' said Trevor, who was too peaceable to be a successful wolf.

'You touched that with your shoulder; I saw,' said Mark, rising on his toes and flexing his arm. A small muscle appeared, just above his elbow.

'You can be wolf, Karen,' said Trevor. He wanted to get on with the game. Karen made off towards the lavatories but Julie intercepted her.

'You're not to go round there, you'll get germs.'

'All right, I'll be wolf again,' said Trevor. Mark danced in among them, his muscle much in evidence.

'Shut you up, Julie Angel, this is my game,' he said. It was at this point that Matthew liked to retire, and normally he would have done so, but as Head Boy it was his job to make peace between boys like Roger and Mark, who didn't mind hitting girls, and girls like Julie and Karen, who didn't mind hitting anyone.

'I'll be shepherd,' he said. 'Trevor's still wolf.' The sheep retreated, growling, to the end of the playground. He had to stay on as shepherd until someone won the position fairly and it was safe to leave them.

He sauntered round to the back of the school and sat on the cloakroom step. Cries of 'Sheep! Sheep!' drifted over the roof, followed by the thunder of feet which made the step shake. The infants played at Sheep and Shepherd several times in a week, but this was the first time that he had ever paid attention to the words although he had played it himself as an infant. They were utter nonsense now but it occurred to him that they must have meant something once. He wondered why they played a game about sheep at all. Most of them had never seen a sheep, except in pictures, any more than they had seen a wolf. There was no longer any wool woven in Norfolk and it must be many years since anyone had grazed sheep in Pallingham, although Ship Loke had once been Sheep Loke, and the bells in the church tower had been paid for with the proceeds of Pallingham wool.

Perhaps the bone in the excavation had come from an antique Norfolk sheep.

It was nearly one o'clock, so he went indoors. Miss Cooper had gone back to the infants' room and Mum was in the kitchen. Mrs Collinge was preparing the afternoon's work.

'Can I see that axe again?' said Matthew. She passed it to him and he held it very gently in both hands. It was so little and vicious, unchanged by time since the day it had failed in the hand of some Stone Age hunter and he had left it lying for Peter's grandad to turn up, six thousand years later. Matthew thought it would have been nice to find the Stone Age man as well, his bones folded neatly in death like the spiders in the toolshed who folded their legs into little wire baskets and died tidily.

He gave back the axe head and longed to be at home and digging. Something must be waiting for him, under the autumn garden.

10. Angels at Large

'How's your archaeology getting along, then?' asked Charlie, next morning, when he met Matthew going for the eggs. Matthew's front tyre was still punctured so he was fetching them on foot. 'Found any more owls yet?'

'I found a bone,' said Matthew. 'That wasn't an owl's, though. Get out of that, Yew.' Yew sank his teeth into Matthew's boot and slew it, still on his foot.

'You'd better get a move on,' said Charlie. 'I'll be over the footpath, time you get back.'

There was only a narrow stretch of field left to plough and the tractor was turned uphill, ready to finish the job. Every night Matthew saw the sweeping headlights as Charlie ploughed in the dark, and every night he thought of Sir Oliver.

'Do you believe in ghosts?' he said.

'I reckon he's haunted,' said Charlie, kicking Yew. 'He've got the devil in him. Do you reckon the parson would say a prayer over him?'

'He might,' said Matthew. 'You should ask him, tomorrow. That's evensong here, this week.' Pallingham shared a vicar with Clipton and Calstead and had no Sunday service, two weeks out of three. 'Mum's doing the flowers, that's how I know.'

'What were all that about ghosts, then?' said Charlie.

'Do you believe in them?'

'Any particular ghost?'

'Have you ever seen Sir Oliver?' said Matthew. 'While you were ploughing?'

'No I haven't,' said Charlie. 'But then, I got other things to look for when I'm ploughing. When I were a boy though, some of us sat out all night in the church to watch for him. Me and my brother Ted, and my cousin Frank and three of the girls sat up in the choir to see him walk through the wall, like we'd been told he would. Must have been mad.'

'Did he come?' asked Matthew. He had expected Charlie to laugh and send him away.

'No he didn't,' said Charlie. 'And we waited till four o'clock in the morning. Never saw a thing.'

'Didn't you try again?' said Matthew. 'I would have.' He knew full well that he would never try it, even once.

'Didn't get the chance,' said Charlie. 'The parson, Mr Hopkins that were, then, he got to hear of it and he took to locking the church on November nights, after that.'

'Mind you,' he added, after a pause. 'That weren't the only reason. Just as we were coming out of the porch I heard this noise.' He looked thoughtful. 'You know what that sound like when you put down a tin pail, and then drop the handle? Well, we heard that, over and over again. Now who'd be doing a thing like that in a churchyard at four in the morning? That were when we left,' said Charlie.

'Is that what armour sounds like?' asked Matthew. He could imagine the noise in his head. It wasn't the sound he had heard on Mrs Bagnall's doorstep but if he thought about it long enough it would be.

'How should I know?' said Charlie. 'I don't wear armour. Come on, Yew.' He whistled to the dog and climbed aboard the tractor. Matthew walked on, along the edge of the dyke, past Charlie's Brussels sprouts, across Fen Street, and up the footpath to the church.

On his right the graves lay in grey dew, bright with chrysanthemums; on his left stood the Howletts' pigsties.

The air was filled with the rollicking sound of pigs kept indoors. As he turned to go through the gate, into the churchyard, a jagged flash of light caught the corner of his eye. It was Charlie, turning the tractor at the top of his field, the ploughshares raised and shining like sharp spoons.

He was in such a hurry to begin digging that he was home again by nine. As he came out of the Brussels sprouts he saw that the old footpath had indeed gone, but Charlie had kindly made a final run with the plough lifted, leaving two wide tyre tracks for Matthew to walk on. This left him no chance to blaze his own trail but it made for faster progress. He would have another opportunity in the spring, after the sugar beet was set.

While he was delivering Mrs Harrison's eggs the Angels' lorry turned in to the loke. He broke into a run in order to be on the premises before the Angels got out of the lorry. Chris was in the cab, with his father. He raised his hand to Matthew and walked to the back of the lorry to lower the tail board. Out spilled Paul, Clive, Julie, and Karen.

'Here's the eggwife,' said Paul.

'Who's that?' said Matthew suspiciously.

'You,' said Paul. 'A midwife delivers babies; an egg-wife delivers eggs.'

'That's rude,' said Julie.

'I've brought my dolly,' said Karen.

'I've brought my doll, too,' said Julie, thrusting it under Matthew's nose. 'My doll's got high heels and a figure. She's called Samantha. Her hair grows, look.' She put her hand under Samantha's plastic raincoat and twiddled a button. Samantha's short, curly hair suddenly became waist-length.

'My dolly can talk,' said Karen, turning her tattooed lady upside down. It moaned faintly.

'You've killed it,' said Paul.

Julie stood Samantha on top of the gate and made her walk up and down. She had blue boots to match the raincoat. Julie turned the button again and the hair shot back into Samantha's head.

'Just like real,' said Julie.

'Let me have a go,' said Matthew. He turned the button and Samantha's hair whizzed in and out at high speed. Then he turned it too far and Samantha had a crew cut. Julie snatched her out of his hand and flounced into the garden, followed as usual by Karen and Clive.

'How's the dig?' asked Paul, standing aside to let Mr Angel and Chris set up the ladder.

'I found a bone,' said Matthew. 'That's round at the back. Come on, I'll show you.'

'How far down was it?' said Paul, looking at the bone with the same interest that Yew would have given it.

'Under the iron. I think I've got all that out now,' said Matthew.

'Blakely Stratum Alpha,' said Paul, patting the heap of iron. 'First Blakely layer,' he translated, for Matthew's benefit. 'You're down to the sub-Blakely strata now. Did you find anything else?'

'Only the bone. What is it?'

'Shoulder of mutton,' said Paul. 'If it's sub-Blakely it can't be one of theirs. Must be just a dead sheep.'

'I thought of that too,' said Matthew. 'But where's the rest of it? Could that be a bit of monk's dinner?'

'Very likely,' said Paul, but he seemed to be laughing. 'I'll get the scythe.' He ducked through the hedge. Matthew collected the coal shovel and began to dig. The edging spade was banned, too good a tool to be employed in idle pursuits.

'Where do you want me to cut now?' asked Paul, returning with the scythe.

'All round the hole,' said Matthew, flattered that Paul should bother to ask him. Paul was merely being polite. He began to work where he had left off, under the oak tree.

'I think you should dig over this way a bit more,' he

said. 'You told me yourself that the priory would be by the wall.'

'I am by the wall.'

'Not by it enough,' said Paul. Matthew saw that he would cut the grass only where he wanted the hole to be.

'I don't want to start another excavation,' he said. 'I've been at this one for days. I can't stop now.'

'You're not finding much though, are you?' said Paul.

'We do stone carving at school,' he added, after a few minutes.

'We do clay modelling at ours,' said Matthew. So what? he added under his breath.

'There's this friend of mine,' said Paul. 'He had a big bit of stone and he started to carve a man out of it and it went wrong, just after he started. I mean, you could see it was going to be a mess – so could he, but he wouldn't stop. He just kept hacking at it. It got smaller and smaller and in the end he just had this nasty little lump. It took him all term too. We only get one hour a week.'

'Didn't he get wrong for wasting all that stone?' asked Matthew. Mrs Collinge made them scrape up even the smallest bits of clay to put back in the bin.

'No. He said it was meant to be like that. He said it was modern art, but our teacher said "Of course it's modern, you fool, you've only just done it." '

'Then what happened?'

'Nothing happened,' said Paul. 'But you're just the same with your hole, only the other way round. It's getting bigger and bigger but you're still going to finish up with nothing and you won't stop, either. You should have left it ages ago.'

This thought had struck Matthew more than once, but he wasn't going to act on it while Paul was watching.

Clive staggered out of the house and approached them.

'I dig,' he said, and tried to take the shovel away from Matthew.

'No,' said Matthew, resisting. 'You don't dig. I dig.'

'I bite,' said Clive. It was like talking to Tarzan. Clive saw something move in the long grass at the foot of the garden and went to investigate.

'Dog,' he said, hopefully.

It was one of Mrs Bagnall's cats, loitering beside the wall. He flung his arms round it and brought it up the garden to show Matthew. It was so long that although he was carrying the front end, the back legs were walking ahead of him and the tail scythed angrily against his shins.

'Come, pussy,' said Clive, steering the cat towards Matthew. It was Tokyo Rose, the half-caste Siamese whose father had been Charlie Hemp's old black tom. It didn't look like a Siamese but it sounded like one, and it yelled all the while Clive was carrying it. Paul left his grass cutting and ran to the rescue.

'Can't you see it doesn't want to be carried,' he said, snatching the cat from his brother, and Clive, who had not thought about the cat's feelings, but only that it was furry, sat down on the grass and ground his hands into the dirt with rage and disappointment.

'Is that my Rose I hear?' asked Mrs Bagnall, looking over the wall. Mr Bagnall reared up from his weeding.

'I thought someone was eating her,' he said, and sank out of sight again.

Paul ran to the wall and looked over.

'Hullo, Sir,' he said, with great gaiety.

'Good God,' said Mr Bagnall, in the voice he usually reserved for the cats. 'Don't I get a moment's peace? I had you for a double period yesterday afternoon and your brother for an hour before that. Hell's bells.'

Paul took this as an invitation to stay and leaned his elbows on the wall.

'You must be Mrs Bagnall. How do you do. I'm Paul Angel. One of Mr Bagnall's favourite students.'

'Good morning, Paul,' said Mrs Bagnall, taking Tokyo Rose and putting her down on her own side of the wall.

'I've been watching you; and you, Matthew. What is it meant to be, an archaeological dig?'

She thought she was joking and Matthew would have let her go on thinking it, but Paul said, 'That's right. Matthew thinks we may find some remains of the priory.'

'How exciting,' said Mrs Bagnall, in a teacherly way. 'And have you found any remains?'

'Nothing to do with the priory, so far,' said Paul. 'Only a lot of old rubbish. But my brother . . .'

'That oaf,' said Mr Bagnall, ripping up dandelions with cruel jerks and leaving all the roots behind.

'My brother says that we ought to leave the rubbish in the ground to be dug up by future generations. Today's rubbish is tomorrow's history, he says.'

'That doesn't surprise me at all,' said Mr Bagnall. 'Judging by the last few essays he's handed in he seems to devote his waking hours to producing history.'

Supercat ambled by and thinking that Mr Bagnall was turning over the earth for his express benefit, began to dig a hole. Mr Bagnall picked him up, tossed him from one hand to the other and thence into the cabbages where he went to ground, his angry tail sticking up like a storm-tossed bullrush.

'Disgusting creature,' said Mr Bagnall. 'Ought to be put down. They all ought to be put down. They ought to be put down a deep, deep hole, a thousand miles away.'

'Don't take any notice of him,' said Mrs Bagnall. 'What do you hope to find?'

'Opinions differ on this,' said Paul, adjusting his conversation to include words that he didn't use when he was talking to Matthew. 'We're operating on different principles. Matthew was looking for bones and foundations, but we're hoping for something more, er, glamorous. Altar plate, perhaps, or coins,' he said, with a gloating hiss on the last word.

Matthew didn't care for the way he said it, nor for the

way he said 'we'. It was a word that did not include him. He left them talking and looked for Clive, in case he was damaging something. He found him in the excavation, watching a worm, his face cushioned on the earth. Deprived of the cat he was consoling himself with the next best thing.

'Good worm, good worm,' he was saying. 'Come here, darling.'

The dig was rained off before lunch time. A gale blew up, forcing Chris and Mr Angel down from the roof, leaving the wind to howl round the bare bones of the rafters. All the Angels crowded into the kitchen to drink tea because Chris had put the ladder through the window at Kingston Villa, which made it too cold for sitting about. They camped round the table, except for Clive who went underneath and untied people's shoe laces. The kitchen steamed like a damp haystack and each rain spot on the window was haloed with mist until the glass clouded over entirely.

'I don't fancy going down to the church in this,' said Mum, wiping a spyhole in the mist. 'How would you like to do that for me, Matthew?'

'I can't arrange flowers,' said Matthew. 'I'll go and pick them for you, if you like, though.' He wanted to get out of the kitchen without seeming rude.

'I'm surprised you've got any flowers to pick,' said Mr Angel. 'Won't they all be finished by now?'

'Cauliflowers,' said Paul. 'They'll look nice on the altar.'

'Chrysanthemums,' said Mum, handing Matthew the kitchen scissors. 'We've had no frost yet: the ones by the hedge are all right, but you'd better cut them all. That'll all be flattened by the wind, else.'

Matthew went out. The wind took him and twirled him as it bowled across the gardens, tearing twigs from the oak tree and unzipping the hedge. He crouched under the apple trees and the rain battered the last leaves over his back as he wrenched at the chrysanthemums with yapping scissors. When he had an armful he butted his way back to the kitchen where a different kind of chaos prevailed. As well as the Angels, the room was full of Dad, home for lunch in a wet oilskin, and Joe Crome, Charlie's uncle from Tokesby, who delivered the papers and had called to collect the week's money.

Matthew squeezed in among them with the chrysanthemums clutched to his chest.

Mr Angel raised his arm with difficulty as if it were on a ratchet, and looked at his watch.

'Time we were off, boys and girls,' he said. 'You take your time, don't you Joe? That's half past nine when you get to ours.'

'This is the end of the round, George,' said Joe.

'I don't complain,' said Dad. 'That give the bad news time to go off the boil. If the world's going to end tonight that'll be over before I've read about it.'

'What about the good news?' asked Chris, oozing sideways while Mum and Dad did a tango round each other to get at the paper money which was kept on the dresser.

'Good news'll keep,' said Dad. 'Here, Janey, I haven't danced with you for years. May I have the next waltz?'

They put their arms round each other and glided into the hall. The Angels looked edgy and stared at the floor.

11. Sir Oliver

Mum put the flowers in a polythene bag to protect them, and Matthew prepared for another walk to the church.

'Why aren't you going on your bike?' asked Dad. 'You can tie the chrysanths to the cross bar.'

'I've got another puncture,' said Matthew.

'Haven't you mended that yet?' said Mum. 'What were you doing all morning?'

'Digging,' said Matthew.

'Hang on,' said Dad. 'I'll give you a lift down there. I'm going through Polthorpe.'

They went out to the car. 'Isn't that about time you saw to that tyre?'

'I don't think that'll take any more mending,' said Matthew. 'That's all over patches, now.'

'That's your own fault,' said Dad. 'I keep telling you not to ride down the loke until they resurface it.'

'I forget.'

'That's still your fault.'

Dad let him out of the Land-Rover by the pigsties. Roger Howlett was leaning over the wall in the rain, sucking a liquorice bootlace. A long black string hung down from his mouth.

'Fishing?' said Matthew. 'Caught anything yet?'

'Here come the bride,' said Roger, eyeing Matthew's flowers. He was too occupied with the bootlace to talk so Matthew left him chewing and went into the churchyard, running with his head bent until he reached the porch and was out of the wind.

Someone was in the porch before him: Mr Catchpole Senior, Peter's grandad, the finder of flint axe-heads and owner of eleven fingers. He was carrying a bunch of evergreens and a spade.

'These are for your Mum, when she come,' he said, pushing the evergreens into Matthew's arms.

'I'm doing the flowers today,' said Matthew.

'Well, you know where everything is,' said Mr Catchpole. He raised the spade and held it over his shoulder like a rifle. 'I've got to see to the moles. That's the Clipton-Calstead match tomorrow.'

Mr Catchpole lived in Myhill Street too, opposite the Bagnalls. He grazed his goat in their ditch. He tended the churchyard and acted as groundsman to the football pitch, which was used by all the villages which had no playing fields of their own. Calstead had a field but it was under water at this time of year.

'What are the moles doing?' asked Matthew.

'Molehills all round the goal,' said Mr Catchpole. 'That's all right when Pallingham's playing but that don't look so good for visitors, moles in goal. They come out of the churchyard. I reckon they find the mixture a bit rich.'

Matthew thought that this was no way to speak of the dead, especially as Mr Catchpole had many relatives in the churchyard himself.

He took the greenery into the church, full of hollow booming as the wind walloped against the roof. Mrs Sadler had already arranged the altar flowers and she had left a can of water by the font. Matthew's flowers had to be placed in two iron stands, on either side of the chancel arch. On top of each stand there was a little zinc tub, filled with dry green sponge to hold the stems in place. It crumbled in his hands and he had to scoop it off the floor in a hymn sheet.

He spent a long time jabbing stalks into the sponge and standing back to admire the effect. The chrysanthemums leaned on each other in the shade of the evergreens as though they had had a riotous night out before coming to church. He pushed the stands up against the archway for support, but as he was moving away someone opened the door and the sudden draught sent the whole lot swaying, dangerously.

Matthew thought that Roger had followed him in to interfere, and shouted 'Shut the door, you silly great nit. That's all blowing away.'

'Please accept my apologies,' said Mr Bagnall, hastily closing the door. 'I thought I was alone.'

Matthew always took great care not to offend Mr Bagnall. Even saying 'Good morning' was liable to make him frown unless it really was a good morning. He wondered how to atone for calling him a silly great nit.

Mr Bagnall walked up the aisle.

'I really am sorry,' he said. 'I had no idea you were in here.'

'I didn't know it was you,' said Matthew. 'I thought that was Roger Howlett.'

'I dare say we're very alike,' said Mr Bagnall. 'When did you take up flower arranging?'

'I'm doing it for Mum. I don't seem to be very good at it though,' said Matthew. 'They wobble when you walk past.'

'Yes,' said Mr Bagnall. 'Things do tend to wobble, when I walk past them.' He was heading for the altar as he spoke, and Matthew walked with him as it seemed rude not to. Mr Bagnall took a key from his pocket and unlocked the vestry door. It was strange to see him here, so much at home. Mrs Bagnall went to church every Sunday, driving to Clipton or Calstead if there was no service at Pallingham, but Mr Bagnall always stayed behind, to threaten the cats in peace, perhaps.

'Coming in?' he asked Matthew, holding the door open.

He seemed a very different person, away from Myhill Street; possibly because there were no cats about.

'Are you allowed in here?' asked Matthew. He had never seen the vestry unlocked.

'Good Lord, no,' said Mr Bagnall. 'I laid out the vicar and pinched his keys. I've got to be out of the country by nightfall.'

'He lent them to you,' said Matthew.

Mr Bagnall sighed. 'You do take the edge off things, don't you? I'm doing some research for an American friend: I have to look at the parish registers.'

'Mr Myhill?' said Matthew. He was the only American that Matthew knew about.

'Who's Mr Myhill?'

'He was an American who came to our house last year, looking for ancestors,' said Matthew. 'He didn't find any, though. I thought that might be him.'

'No,' said Mr Bagnall. 'My friend's name is Morgenstern. I don't think he has any ancestors in Pallingham.' He selected another key and opened a wooden chest, full of books.

'Registers,' he said. 'What a mess.' He took out a thick volume, apparently bound in cobwebs. 'You might like this. You're interested in old buildings, aren't you?'

Matthew took the book, amazed that Mr Bagnall should care about what interested him.

'Paul told you that, didn't he? Him and Chris said I shouldn't let you know what I was doing because you couldn't stand damned amateurs digging things up.'

'I don't think you're in quite the same class as Lord Elgin,' said Mr Bagnall. 'And I don't honestly think that there's anything to find, let alone damage. It would be nice if you did, though. There's very little known about it.'

'About the priory? Nobody cares anyway. I can't get anyone to tell me about it,' said Matthew. 'That's the same with Sir Oliver. They say he's only a story.'

'He was real enough,' said Mr Bagnall. 'I can show you that. In fact, it was his priory.'

'He built it? Like Sir Robert built the church?'

'Built and endowed it,' said Mr Bagnall. 'That is, he left a certain amount of money for its upkeep, but the money ran out and his monks were a bad lot. When the Bishop's commissioners examined the prior and brethren he found them guilty of incontinence. You don't understand that, do you? They'd been living it up and cooking the books.'

'I didn't know monks were like that,' said Matthew, recalling the bespectacled bore in the bus station.

'Things were different then,' said Mr Bagnall. 'People became monks because they had nothing else to do. When the commissioners returned the following year they found the place empty.' He took the book from Matthew and opened it. 'Here we are. "The religious persons of the same are gone and the chattels wasted and spoiled." This chap thinks they took everything they could carry and decamped. Now, he was writing a hundred and fifty years ago and nothing's come to light since. If the brothers Angel imagine that they're going to find altar plate and coins they've got another think coming.'

'Good,' said Matthew. 'That's my hole, after all. I suppose Sir Oliver goes to look at his priory when he walks. Why does he start here?'

'That's the mystery,' said Mr Bagnall. 'After he died he was buried in the priory but when the monks left it began to fall down, assisted, no doubt, by the local lads who borrowed the stone for their own desirable residences. Sir Robert, our Sir Robert, I mean, brought the bones back and put up a tomb in the church that he was building: the one we're standing in now. Presumably Oliver was quite happy where he was, that's why he keeps trying to get back, along the old causeway.'

'What's that?'

'In those days it was the main road between Hoxenham and Pallingham. Your footpath follows the same route. When the wheat's growing you can see the outlines of the old causeway from the top of the church tower. Remind me, in spring, and I'll take you up the church tower to look.'

'So that's why he sticks to the footpath,' said Matthew. He was beginning to feel sorry for Sir Oliver, fiddled by his monks and chivvied from grave to grave after his death. 'Where's his grave gone? Is that the mystery?'

'Not quite,' said Mr Bagnall. 'We know where his grave went. Robert put it in the Lady Chapel, in the North Aisle.'

'There's no chapel now.'

'No. The roof fell in with monotonous regularity,' said Mr Bagnall. 'Word went round that Sir Oliver was resting uneasy and shaking the foundations. By the time this chap wrote his book, the place was in such a mess that there was talk of demolishing it. It wasn't quite propped up with old bedsteads but it looked bad, and they took it down, about three years later. That was the mystery. When they opened the tomb – no Sir Oliver.'

'How did he get out?'

'You tell me,' said Mr Bagnall. 'But he's got no grave now. He walks.'

Matthew looked out of the vestry door at Sir Robert dozing on his tomb, still looking smug in spite of having no ankles.

'He's still there,' said Mr Bagnall. 'But even he's in reduced circumstances. Look at this.' He turned a page or two in the book and laid it on the vicar's desk where Matthew could see it. There was a picture, a black engraving with brown freckles. Sir Robert lay on his slab complete with nose and ankles and clasping a sword. 'He had a severed head for a pillow in those days. Charming chap.' There was a finicking stone canopy over the tomb that looked as if it had been crocheted. Underneath it said, *Icy gist Monsver Robert Coningbrook Fondevr de cette Eglise et*

Dame Johanne sa Compagne auxi Priez Dieu de leur Almes eit Merci.

'What does all that mean?' asked Matthew. It didn't look like any language in particular, especially not English, but he could read the words 'Robert Coningbrook' quite well.

'That's what was written round the tomb,' said Mr Bagnall. 'It's all worn away now but it was French, or at least, French as she was spoken in those days. It means, more or less: Here lies Sir Robert Coningbrook, founder of this church, and his wife Dame Joan, also. Pray God have mercy on their souls.'

'Why French? They were English, weren't they?'

'They were Normans. None of your British rubbish,' said Mr Bagnall.

'That says something else on the tomb now,' said Matthew. 'Carved on Sir Robert. Gilbert d'Arcy Sinclair 1839.'

'I know,' said Mr Bagnall. 'It's beautifully done too, must have taken him hours. He was a Victorian vandal. If he were alive today he'd be spraying his name on lavatory walls with an aerosol: Gilbert d'Arcy Sinclair Rules O.K.?'

'Is that Sir Oliver?' asked Matthew, looking at the next picture. It was much smaller. Sir Oliver lay with his little dog at his feet and there was no canopy to protect him. All it said underneath was, *Priez pour les Almes de Monsver Oliver de Hoxenha et Dame Julian sa Femme.*

'Pray for the souls of Sir Oliver of Hoxenham and Dame Julian, his wife,' said Mr Bagnall. 'Myhill Street was in Hoxenham, then, only it wasn't called Myhill Street until recently. You know, there wasn't much left of his tomb even then. At one time his helmet and crest hung above it. The crest was rather nice, I think. A pun on his name. It was an owl. Oliver the owl, sitting on a crescent moon. I suppose he borrowed the moon from the Saracens; he was a crusader in his youth.'

'How do you know all this?' asked Matthew.

'Your Sir Oliver's quite famous outside his own village,' said Mr Bagnall. 'He was a verray parfit, gentil knight, and now I'm sure you don't know what I'm talking about.' Suddenly he was the old Mr Bagnall again, cat-crusher in chief to the village of Pallingham. 'I've got work to do. You'd better take yourself off.' Matthew backed out of the vestry and left him snarling into the parish registers.

So Charlie's owl was Sir Oliver's owl, and the priory was Sir Oliver's priory, and Sir Oliver, with nowhere to rest and no monument to remember him by, was his own memorial, walking the causeway in the long November nights.

12. Angels *in situ*

The Angels had gone when he reached home, and Mum was making bread in the kitchen. A bowl of flour stood warming on the stove and beside it was a jug full of yeast. He looked to see what kind she was using. Fresh yeast rose in the jug with an ebullient fizz, dried yeast worked with silent belches rising from the depths. It was dried yeast today and he stood and watched the surface plop and shudder until all the barm had risen to the top.

'Flowers all right?' asked Mum, and she poured the yeasty liquid into the flour, working them into a dough.

'I think so,' said Matthew, trying not to see the drunken chrysanthemums in the chancel. 'Has everyone gone home?'

'George is still next door,' said Mum. 'But he sent the children home with Chris. That was too cold for them to be in that house.'

'Why does he bring them, then?' said Matthew, remembering that there was some mystery about this. Mum was kneading the bread and didn't answer him.

'They left a message for you,' she said, after a while. 'Would you like to go over to tea at Hoxenham tomorrow? Someone's having a birthday but I can't recall who.'

'Do I have to?' said Matthew. 'I don't really want to go to tea with them. They get all over the place. Look at them here. You wouldn't think that was our house at all.'

'They're all right, poor little devils,' said Mum.

'Not poor,' said Matthew. 'Not Karen and Julie. Just little devils.'

'No, not Karen and Julie,' said Mum. 'Anyway, they're good fun. You go to tea and have a nice time. You'd better take chocolates as we don't know who it's for.'

'Myhill Street used to be in Hoxenham,' said Matthew.

'Well, I'm glad that's not now. Their rates are higher than ours. Where are you going?'

'I thought I'd go and dig for a bit,' said Matthew.

'You can't go and dig in this weather, don't be silly.'

'That's stopped raining.'

'No,' said Mum. 'You go upstairs and get on with your work for school. Mrs Collinge will want to see that, Monday.'

Matthew went upstairs. Mum and Mrs Collinge thought he was working at some pictures for the history chart, but he had done nothing. He sat on the bed and thought about Sir Oliver and the owl. After a long time he understood what a pun was.

He dug all Sunday morning and found a brick. Paul had made sure that he dug towards the wall by cutting the grass on that side of the hole and nowhere else. After lunch he had to tidy himself for the party.

When he arrived at the Angels' estate he saw that he needn't have bothered. Everything was going on as usual: Paul in gum boots, Chris in the garage, Clive on a heap of rubble, lurching from side to side and screeching, whereby Matthew understood that the rubble was a racing car. Paul was standing beside him, providing a rapid commentary.

'They're coming out of the straight now and Clive Angel in the Hard-Core Special is in the lead – he's pulling away – no, I can see smoke – he's in trouble . . .'

Clive jumped off the heap of rubble, walked to the rear and kicked it.

'Filler cap,' he said.

'That wouldn't cause smoke,' said Matthew.

'He doesn't understand,' said Paul. 'He just repeats

what he hears Chris say.' Clive tore up some grass, stuffed it into a broken drainpipe and climbed into his car.

'Keep going,' said Paul. 'You'll win.' He walked up to the house with Matthew.

'Is that a present you've got there?'

'Yes. Who's it for?'

'Me,' said Paul, taking it. 'I was thirteen on Friday. The others are watching telly. Come on in.'

They entered the house via the bathroom and went into the living-room. It was quite dark inside, with the curtains drawn. Julie and Karen were sitting in front of the television.

'Just like trolls,' said Paul. 'One shaft of light and they'd turn to stone.'

'What's a troll?'

There were two other people in the room. 'Nan and Grandad,' said Paul, by way of introduction. Matthew smiled towards them in the darkness. He could hardly say 'How do you do, Nan and Grandad.'

'You call the boys in, Paul,' said Nanny Angel. 'Tea's laid in the other room. We'll have that as soon as you're all clean.'

Paul returned to the bathroom and yelled through the open door. Chris came in to wash. Clive charged straight through, into the living-room, and hurled himself at the television set. He ran his fingers over the control panel, switching off the sound and altering the colour so that the ballerinas on the screen turned to silently jigging green grasshoppers.

'Come you off that,' said Nanny Angel, bearing him into the bathroom. 'Here, Chris, get some of the dirt off him before tea.'

They settled round the table in the next room. Nanny Angel sat at the head, dealing out slices of flan like a croupier.

'Cream thickens the blood,' said Nanny Angel, pouring a generous amount over everyone's plate except her own.

They started to eat. Grandad Angel took his plate back to the living-room and switched on the television again.

'Clive's got his arm in the food,' said Karen.

'Take your arm out of the food, Clive,' said Chris, automatically, without looking up. He was reading *Practical Car Conversion* under the table. Nanny Angel lined up the cups in front of her and began to pour tea, starting at one end and swishing along to the other without raising the spout between cups, so that much of the tea went into the saucers. The Angels merely tipped the tea back into the cups without comment, except for Clive who upended his cup in the saucer and drank out of that.

'Clive's drinking out of his saucer,' said Karen.

'Don't drink out of your saucer, Clive,' said Chris.

Clive blew a bubble and continued to drink out of the saucer. Matthew thought they might be invited to wash up afterwards, but Nanny Angel joined Grandad in front of the television and the others left the table, still eating. Matthew waited to see where Julie and Karen went and then moved off in the other direction. Paul followed with a handful of sandwiches.

'Pilchard or cheese and tomato?' he said, offering them to Matthew. 'Let's go and see what Frankenstein's up to.'

Matthew thought he was talking about a television programme but they were heading for the garage. Frankenstein was Chris and his monster was the car parked over the inspection pit. He was building it with pieces taken from other cars. Beside it stood an old Ford Zodiac with *Fat Sally* painted across the lid of the boot.

'We're taking her banger racing next year,' said Paul, patting Fat Sally on the roof. 'When we get an engine inside her.'

Chris looked out of the inspection pit. 'I've got your present here,' he said, and pushed it out onto the ground, wrapped in newspaper. Paul knelt down in a pool of sump oil and unwrapped it.

'An exhaust manifold,' said Paul. 'Just what you wanted. How did you guess?'

'Got it cheap,' said Chris. 'It fell off the back of a friend. I'm going to fit it tonight.' He withdrew, taking the manifold.

That was the end of Paul's birthday present.

Matthew thought, personally, that Paul was having a lousy birthday.

'He's taken your present,' he said.

'We share things,' said Paul, defensively. 'And he did buy it. Last week he took the steering wheel out of Fat Sally and put it in his. Have a sandwich.'

There was a slithering sound behind them. Matthew turned round and saw Clive falling out of the Hard-Core Special. He hit his chin on it and stood in the desolate dust, crying for his mother. Chris came out of the garage and picked him up.

13. First Frost

Two rival games were in session at opposite ends of the playground and in the middle Peter and Roger were practising Japanese methods of mayhem, high-kicking like ballet dancers.

Peter crouched on the ground, his knees level with his ears, and swayed from side to side.

'My brother taught me this one,' he said. 'But you have to take a vow never to use it because that kills, instantly. You'll have to lean down a bit or I can't reach.' He sprang up and wrapped his feet round Roger's neck. Roger did not die and Peter fell heavily on the back of his head. He retired to try again and Matthew, seeing that he was not going to have a corpse on his hands, continued his stroll round the playground. Behind the dustbins he found Mark Catchpole, kneeling on the ground and stuffing something into an airbrick.

'You shouldn't do that,' said Matthew. 'Those airbricks are meant to have holes in. The wall will get damp, else.'

'I'll take them out, after play,' said Mark. 'I'm a terrorist. I'm planting a bomb.' He pointed to three other little ones who were squinnying round the corner, trying to stay out of sight. 'They're the security forces.'

'That's horrible,' said Matthew. 'What do you want to do that for?'

'I'm going to blow up the school,' said Mark. 'That's an

army post.' He noticed that Matthew still looked disgusted. 'That's not a real bomb, only mud and acorns.'

'Why do you want to blow anyone up?' said Matthew. 'We don't have any troubles here.'

'That's only a game,' said Mark. 'Like on telly.'

'That's not a game on telly,' said Matthew.

'This is,' said Mark, gently, and backed away, keeping close to the ground. The security forces broke cover and charged after him, firing with rulers. Matthew saw that it was no more than the usual game of pursuer and pursued. As you could be a sheep or a wolf without ever having seen either, so you could be a terrorist without ever having seen a bomb. In a hundred years, perhaps, they would still be playing at bombs and never knowing why: still fighting over whose turn it was to be the terrorist.

He started after them but Mrs Collinge saw him go by and called him in. At first he thought of turning deaf for on present form Mrs Collinge was unlikely to say anything that he wanted to hear, but Mrs Collinge waved and he couldn't get away with being blind as well. She was standing by the history charts, and tapped Matthew's with a piece of chalk.

'Are you ever going to put anything on this?' she asked, as he crossed the room. 'You seem to have lost interest in it altogether.'

Matthew felt like telling her that he had never been interested in it in the first place, but he could see that this was not what he was expected to say. Mrs Collinge was looking sorrowful instead of angry so he had to be nice about it.

'I just can't think of anything to put on it,' he said, also sounding sorrowful, to keep up his part of the act. 'We don't live in an historic house.'

'Half the people here live in council houses,' said Mrs Collinge. 'You can't get much less historic than that, but they've all managed to find something.'

Matthew didn't think that this was a fair comparison. The council estate was built in the grounds of the Old Hall, another of Sir Robert's efforts. Wherever you looked there was something old in view, and it was easy to see which of the history charts belonged to people from the estate. They had all drawn the same things.

'Even a council house will be historic one day,' said Mrs Collinge.

It was the same old story. Everything was going to be history if you waited long enough.

Mum left a row of tea towels on the line overnight, and next morning they hung still and stiff, starched with frost. Matthew tried to take them down and the frozen pegs bit his fingers.

'Don't fold them, they'll crack,' said Mum.

Matthew tweaked the corner of one of the towels. 'Will they really?'

'I don't know,' said Mum. 'But my mother always said they would and I've never liked to find out.'

'Let's try it.'

'Oh no you don't,' said Mum. 'Tea towels cost a fortune. You take them indoors.'

'This one's got a big hole in it.'

'No.'

Matthew stood the towels in the sink.

'First frost,' said Mum. 'I'll make the cake and the puddings tomorrow. I'll go into Polthorpe after lunch to get the fruit.'

Every year, after the first frost, Mum made the Christmas cake and the Christmas puddings, as her mother had done it before her. It was a ritual.

'Suppose we don't get a frost before Christmas?' said Matthew, each time they had a mild autumn.

When he came home from school on Friday the kitchen smelled of strong drink. The puddings were made from a rare old recipe with rum in it. There was sherry in the cake and brandy in the mince meat. The air was so spirituous that it might ignite with a blue flash if anyone struck a match. Dad, home early for his Friday tea, was eating it off the corner of the dresser because the table was crowded with bowls and packets, standing among spilled raisins.

'Come and have a wish,' said Mum, holding out the wooden spoon.

Matthew reckoned he was getting beyond such things but he took the spoon, dug it into the mixture, and wished. There was only one thing that he could wish for – that he would find something in the excavation, and quickly. He had one picture for his history chart, a very bad drawing of Kingston Villa with the roof off, so bad that it was still in his desk and not on the chart. Even Roger Howlett had done more than he had. His chart, which hung next to Matthew's, was covered in notes and sketches. Some of them were very strange but at least they were there, and Roger, after all, was the school nuisance. Matthew felt that he owed it to them to be a nuisance all the time.

'Finished?' said Mum, taking the spoon from him. 'That was a record wish, wasn't it?' She began to transfer the pudding mixture from the bowl to the row of white basins on the dresser. The black, iron cauldron which was kept in the larder during the rest of the year was already bubbling on the stove. The pudding basins were capped with foil, swaddled in white cloths and lowered on strings into the cauldron. There were muffled thuds as they bounced in the boiling water and tipsy steam escaped from under the lid.

The puddings were not for this Christmas but for next. They would have to sit darkly in their basins at the back of the cupboard and mature like fine cheese. This year they would eat last year's puddings, and last year they had eaten puddings made the year before that.

'Did you have time to wash my kit?' asked Matthew. 'We're playing at Polthorpe tomorrow.'

'Big match?' said Dad. 'I might find time to come down and watch.'

'No, that's only their second eleven,' said Matthew. 'They won't field their first eleven against us.' There weren't enough junior boys to make up a team at Pallingham, so they joined forces with Calstead School. The infants would willingly have joined the team, but they all watched football on television and spent so much time engaged in fancy footwork that they rarely got near the ball.

14. Brass Effrontery

Matthew was digging in his football boots. After the match Mr Overton, the headmaster from Calstead, had dropped him at the end of the loke instead of taking him back to school. This saved him having to walk home again but he had left his shoes in the cloakroom where they would have to stay until Monday.

It had not been a very good game. Polthorpe had won, six-nil, and two of those had been own goals. Matthew was sorry about the own goals, but not too sorry because he was the goalie and at least he hadn't been so responsible for those. It was the other four that worried him.

On the way home Peter Catchpole had refused to speak to him. Peter was the captain and a devoted supporter of Norwich City. Most of his clothes were green and yellow and even his bike was painted to match. As he dug, Matthew treated himself to an action replay to see where he had gone wrong, but he knew, without having to think about it. He was simply too slow and all the time his mind had been on the history charts. He was getting to the stage where he felt sick when he remembered them.

He stopped work and sat down on the edge of the excavation. As Paul had predicted, the rain had made the ground like a pudding and the digging was beginning to hurt his back. He stirred the pudding with the coal shovel and made another wish, for dry weather.

Round the edge of the hole lay all the things he had

found, airing in the wind. Julie came down the garden and began to kick them about.

'Why do you want these filthy old things?' she asked. 'Your hand's bleeding. You'll get lockjaw.'

'No I won't. Get your feet out,' said Matthew. Julie climbed down into the pit.

'That's like a little house in here. You could put a roof on and camp in it.'

'Get out,' said Matthew. He leaned down and grabbed her by the hair. Julie began to scream, slowly, conserving her breath for the final shriek. Matthew expected Karen to arrive and attack him; instead Paul came out of the house.

'Don't do that,' he said, pushing Matthew aside.

'He pulled my hair,' said Julie. 'I'm going to tell my Dad.'

'Off you go then,' said Paul, and grasped a handful of hair himself.

'Just helping you up,' he explained. Matthew recalled that only Angels were allowed to manhandle other Angels.

'What have you got today?' asked Paul, searching among the muddy lumps at the pit's edge. 'I haven't seen this before.'

'I got that out just now,' said Matthew. 'I haven't looked at that properly yet. It's only a bit of old metal.'

Paul picked up a stick and gouged the mud out of the crevices. 'Here, come and have a look at this, Chris.'

Chris was on the lean-to, carefully removing a colony of house leeks that were growing among the tiles, before he stripped the roof. In response to Paul's shout he climbed down and came towards them carrying the house leeks in his hands, all in one clump.

'You'd better put these back when we've finished,' he said, passing the house leeks to Matthew. 'They keep the lightning away.'

Matthew put the house leeks down quickly, for they were sharp. They sat in the grass like a green hedgehog.

'Look what Matthew's found,' said Paul. 'Mind you, he didn't know he'd found it. Thought it was rubbish, didn't you,' he said to Matthew.

'No I didn't. I never had time to look at it properly,' said Matthew, not caring to admit that he had indeed thought it was rubbish.

'This is very interesting,' said Chris, turning the object every way. He took out a handkerchief and scrubbed at it. 'It's the thermostat off a Morris 10 – you know, Paul. The ones that were put on the radiator caps.'

Matthew stood up to look. The thermostat was two glass discs in a circular brass frame, with an indicator needle between them. From the frame grew a long brass stalk.

'That's the sensor unit,' said Chris, stroking the stalk. 'The part that went down into the radiator. The driver could see the dial from inside the car.'

'Is it rare?' said Matthew. His wish had been answered although not, perhaps, in quite the way he had hoped. Sir Oliver had never driven a Morris 10.

'It's extinct,' said Chris. 'They went out of production in nineteen thirty-seven.'

'Hmm,' said Paul. 'At that rate, we ought to get down to the thirteenth century in about ten years' time. Give me a shout when you get there, Matthew, and I'll come and help.'

'My Dad would like to see that,' said Matthew. 'He knows about old cars.' He held out his hand for it.

'Keep digging,' said Chris. 'There may be some more of it, somewhere. I'll just put this in the cab,' and he took it away.

'That's mine,' said Matthew. 'I found it.'

'You didn't want it. You're looking for bones, aren't you?'

'You said you were looking for coins,' said Matthew. 'Why do you want it? That's mine.'

'It's on loan,' said Paul, soothingly. 'I was joking about the coins. You knew that.'

'And the altar plate?'

'Of course I was.'

'Mr Bagnall said you'd never find anything like that,' said Matthew. 'What are you looking for, then?'

'Anything that comes up,' said Paul. 'It's all interesting. You've got another spade in your toolshed, haven't you? I'll get it.'

'I'm not allowed to use that any more,' said Matthew, when Paul came back with the spade.

'Ah, but I am,' said Paul. 'I asked your Mum.'

Chris returned with a builder's trowel. 'A real archaeologist doesn't dig, he scrapes,' he said.

'We're going to a museum on Thursday,' said Matthew. 'I shall know what to look out for, then.'

'We've got something doing on Thursday,' said Paul. 'What is it, Chris?'

Chris took a little diary from his pocket and consulted it. 'Eclipse of the moon,' he said. 'Begins about eight, if you want to watch it, Matthew. Let's hope it stays clear, it's total this time.'

'We're going to watch it from the inspection pit,' said Paul. 'If Chris can get the car out of the way.'

'I'll try and start her tomorrow,' said Chris. 'Wasn't it Aristotle who thought that the stars looked bigger if you sat down a hole to observe them?'

'Who was Aristotle?' asked Matthew. Perhaps he was another Angel.

'Ancient Greek,' said Chris. 'It's strange, isn't it? You still get Greeks called Aristotle and Socrates.'

'Let's have that trowel, a minute,' said Paul. 'It must be embarrassing to be thick and Greek and called Socrates.'

'Who was Socrates?' asked Matthew.

'Like being thick and Jewish and called Solomon.'

'Or thick and English and called Shakespeare,' said Paul.

'Dad used to know a brickie called Shakespeare,' said Chris.

'William?'

'No, Raymond.'

'That doesn't sound right, Raymond Shakespeare,' said Paul. 'It's like Bruce van Beethoven or Melvyn Sebastian Bach.'

'Everyone called him Shakes,' said Chris.

Matthew, ignored, crouched at the bottom of the pit, while the cat's cradle of conversation ran back and forth over his head. He could tell that it was meant to be funny from the smiles in their voices, but the jokes went over his head too.

Mum called through the hedge that there was tea brewed for anyone who wanted it. The door of Kingston Villa burst open and Angels issued out. Mr Angel and Mr John Angel came down from the roof and Charlie Hemp, who was rabbiting in the field, looked over the wall and asked if he might come too.

Chris and Paul followed the others, but Matthew stayed in the hole, unable to face the overflowing kitchen. When he next raised his head he saw Mr Bagnall leaning on the wall at the corner. Alongside him sat Minnie, now perfectly spherical and fluffed up like a hen in a high wind.

'Airing her musty fur,' said Mr Bagnall. 'Aren't you going to have tea with your nice new friends?'

'You can hardly get into the kitchen when they're here,' said Matthew. 'I'll have mine when they all come out again.'

'Don't be too hard on them,' said Mr Bagnall. 'I think they feel they have to stick together these days.'

'Why?' said Matthew. 'They do what they like. Everybody lets them do what they like. Everybody likes them.'

'Everybody?'

'Mum and Dad.'

'I suppose that is just about everybody,' said Mr Bagnall. 'But I don't think you'll find they like them so very much. They're sorry for them.'

'Sorry!' said Matthew. 'They're doing all right on it, then.'

Mr Bagnall cleared his throat. 'We are not alone,' he said, and pointed over Matthew's shoulder. Clive was standing by the hole, looking down into it.

'All gone,' he said, puzzled.

'They're at mine,' said Matthew. 'Having tea. Do you want some?'

'Tea. I have,' said Clive. He held out his hand and Matthew led him towards the hedge.

'Goodbye,' said Mr Bagnall. Matthew turned back. The light was bad but he had the distinct impression that Mr Bagnall was stroking Minnie.

The light was very bad.

'Where did you get to?' asked Mr Angel as Matthew ushered Clive into the kitchen. 'I thought he was with you, Paul.'

'I thought he was with Julie,' said Paul.

'Well, you keep an eye on him,' said Mr Angel. 'He'll be out on the road next.'

Mum gave Matthew the green mug which he hated because it made the tea taste foggy. Yew and Charlie were propped up by the sink, Charlie drinking from the Friday teacup and Yew from the washing-up bowl.

'He like the detergent,' said Charlie.

Clive sat on the floor and gave Yew's tail a tentative tug. Yew got down from the sink and sat on his lap, his middle across Clive's knees and the rest of him spread out on either side. Clive's mouth opened and all the air came out of him in a startled wuff. He put his arms round Yew's neck and they collapsed together against the skirting board.

'Here, come you off of that,' said Charlie. 'He'll crush him to death.' He reached out for Yew's collar but Clive tightened his hold.

'Good dog,' he said, ever so quietly.

'I should leave him there,' said his father. 'At least we know where he is.'

15. Museum Pieces

Mrs Collinge borrowed the minibus from Polthorpe School and before lunch she backed it up against the school gate and they practised getting into it. They had to make themselves very thin indeed and it took a long time to re-arrange people so that the narrowest ones were in the right places on the narrowest seats. Matthew, Peter, and Roger were the broadest so they sat in the front with Mrs Collinge.

Miss Cooper came out after lunch to help squeeze them all in. She was staying behind with the little ones who were going to move into the junior classroom for the afternoon and bake lumpy cakes in the school oven.

Matthew went to Norwich once a year for Christmas shopping. He went on the bus with Mum, a long and enter-taining journey because the bus took to the lanes, stopping at secluded broad-side villages where no one got on. Mrs Collinge went straight down the main road and they arrived in half an hour, not nearly as long as the bus took, but still plenty of time to serenade Anne Lilley.

> Happy birthday to you,
> Squashed tomatoes and stew.
> Bread and butter in the gutter
> Happy birthday to you.

It took another half hour to get through the traffic and into the car park. They unfolded themselves and climbed out of the minibus. Mrs Collinge arranged them in twos with Matthew and Anne Lilley at the back to keep the line from straggling.

The Castle Museum, a big, square biscuit tin of a building, stood above them on its hill, but they were not going there. Mrs Collinge led them down narrow streets and alleyways until they came to a wide doorway in a wall. She fanned them through it with flapping hands and they found themselves standing in a courtyard.

'This is Stranger's Hall,' she said, backing them up against the wall. 'It's a very old house and it's been beautifully cared for. Don't touch anything. Roger! You must all stay together, but if anyone does get left behind, stay where you are. We'll come back for you. Don't come looking for us or you're sure to get lost.'

They followed her up the steps to the front door.

'What's that funny smell?' said Julie, looking round for something to complain about.

'Beeswax,' said Mrs Collinge. 'They use it to polish wood. Before modern polishes were invented, there was nothing else to use.'

Matthew made a note of this in his work book. He thought it would be rather pleasant to have a museum devoted entirely to smells. This wasn't his idea of a museum at all. He had expected glass cases full of treasure: rings and buckles and coins and stuffed animals, perhaps a skeleton or two with interesting head wounds . . .

But as Mrs Collinge had said, this was just a very old house.

Each room represented a different time in history, starting with a terrible red Victorian drawing-room, so full of furniture that walking through it would have been like walking through a maze only they couldn't walk through it. All the rooms had thick ropes across the doorways in case anyone sneaked in for a quiet nap on the furniture, perhaps. One little room was locked and had to be viewed through a glass panel. According to the notice beside it all the furniture in that room was made of papier maché.

Mrs Collinge told them that papier maché was pulped paper that dried very hard.

Paper furniture?

Matthew went back for another look and found that the others had gone on without him. He didn't want to be the one that Mrs Collinge had to come back for. It was the kind of thing that seemed to be happening to him lately.

Stranger's Hall began to live up to its name, a big trap for people who didn't know their way about. He took a wrong turning and found himself in a room possessed by clothes: clothes to be christened in, clothes to be married in, clothes to wear to a funeral. The sort of clothes that looked as if once in them you would never get out. They were all displayed on stiff people without heads, and were so stiff themselves that they too might have been made of papier maché.

He escaped from the menacing clothes and came upon the worst room of all. It was full of toys in glass cases. They were the oldest, saddest toys in the world, toys to frighten you into growing up. Dolls with pale, pinched faces and dingy dresses, endless lines of wooden animals queuing in front of an ark that they would never get into, a painted cart full of teddy bears: wizened, withered teddy bears, moulting and bald teddy bears, all nursing a secret sorrow, who had been told to get into the cart and look as if they were having a good time.

Matthew had never had much time for teddy bears. His own was in the attic and he hadn't seen it for years, nor wanted to, but now he longed to smash the glass, overturn the cart and tell them to run for it. He had a vision of all the liberated bears scrambling out of the cart and rampaging down the stairs, disturbing the public.

He left the toys and hurried down corridors and staircases, looking for the rest of the class. Away in the distance he could hear familiar voices and rounding a corner he ran into Mrs Collinge.

She was wearing the expression she kept especially for him, these days.

'I didn't expect to lose you,' she said. 'You're supposed to be keeping the others together. When I said that people who got left behind were to wait I meant you as much as anyone else.'

They trailed through more rooms until they came out in the entrance hall where the class was waiting. There was a certain amount of nudging going on. Julie said loudly, 'Matthew got lost,' and everyone else said 'Aaaaah' to show how sorry they were.

'I think we have enough time left to look in the cellars,' said Mrs Collinge, and they all went through a door and down steps to the passages under the house.

'How did you manage that?' said Roger, in his ear.

'What?'

'How did you manage to get left behind?'

'I didn't manage it,' said Matthew. 'I went back to look at that paper furniture and when I turned round you'd all gone.'

'Oh,' said Roger. 'I tried to get lost but they kept coming back for me.'

They left Stranger's Hall and filed back along the narrow lanes to the Bridewell Museum.

'What's bridewell?' said Anne. 'Somewhere you get married?'

'It used to be a prison,' said Mrs Collinge, and Roger began to drag his feet like a man with a ball and chain.

'All stay in line, this time,' said Mrs Collinge, on the way in. 'Go straight up the stairs and wait for me there. You too, Matthew. In fact, you'd better go first, to lead the way.'

Matthew knew that this was not why he had to go first

and so did the others. They stood back and bowed as he went to the head of the line.

Stranger's Hall had shown how people lived at home. The Bridewell showed how they lived at work: room after room lined with eel traps and looms, ploughs and sewing machines. One room was full of elderly shoes, ancestors of the ones that were still made in Norwich. It didn't seem possible that any of the shoes had ever contained feet. They were shrivelled little things, the kind of shoes that vampire bats might wear.

They went downstairs again, among wagons and wind-mills and the faces of people outside in Bridewell Alley, looking in.

In one corner was a cabinet full of bottles. Matthew paused to have a look because the bottles had a bright, fantastic appearance, quite unlike the bottles that lived in the sideboard at home, but the others piled up behind him and he had to move on.

Mrs Collinge caught him up.

'Was there something you wanted to see, Matthew?'

He shook his head.

'I don't want you to miss things,' she said. 'So long as I know where you are.'

He knew that she was trying to be kind but it was too late and he got an angry sort of pleasure from walking away. In the entire afternoon, the bottles were the only things that he had wanted to see. Bottles, after all, were the kind of things that got thrown out and were therefore the kind of things that might be dug up.

On the way to the minibus they passed the castle again.

'What sort of a museum is that?' asked Peter.

'They have all sorts of things in there,' said Mrs Collinge. 'There's an art gallery, and a section on natural history, and archaeology: suits of armour, mummies, pottery. It's really half a dozen museums rolled into one.'

Matthew, eavesdropping, trailed again, kicking himself

across the car park. The whole horrible afternoon lay waste behind him. He had been in the wrong museums.

'You'll get lead poisoning if you do that,' said Julie.

'No I won't,' said Matthew, pushing the pencil further into his mouth.

'Your fingernails will turn blue and fall out.'

'They don't put lead in pencils any more.'

'Why are they called lead pencils then?' said Julie. 'You don't know everything.' She amended this. 'You don't know anything.'

They were thin on the ground this afternoon. The junior boys had gone off to play a match against Clipton and Matthew had been dropped from the team.

'I'm sorry,' said Peter, trying to look it. 'I daren't risk that. We'll be relegated at this rate.'

'Don't be daft,' said Matthew. 'Relegated from what?'

'I mean, no one won't want to play with us, soon. We're a joke. We've played seven games this term, lost six, drawn one, won nothing. We've scored three goals in seven games.'

'You can't blame me for that,' said Matthew. 'I'm the goalie.'

'Were the goalie,' Peter corrected him. 'I can't let the team go downhill like this.'

'But who will you substitute? No one else is big enough.'

'I have conferred with Calstead,' said Peter, who studied First Division managers in his spare time, 'and we've decided to play Trevor Lilley. He's come on a lot this season.'

'But he's hopeless,' said Matthew. 'He falls over.'

'That's one way of stopping the ball,' said Peter, nastily.

'You're in a bad mind,' said Matthew. 'That doesn't matter whether we win or not, does it? Not the way we play.'

This was the wrong thing to say.

'I wish Darren was back,' said Peter.

Matthew thought guiltily about Darren, as he sat with

the girls. It was a good thing that he had not accepted Darren's bet because he had not thought about him, much less written to him, since Darren went into hospital. The class had sent a card and some sweets but Matthew had promised to write personally. He tore a page from his arithmetic book and began to compose a letter.

'You're not allowed to do that,' said Julie.

'Go and tell on me then,' said Matthew, but it was not necessary. Mrs Collinge was standing behind him, reading the note out loud, over his shoulder. '"Dear Darren Catchpole have drop me from the team I'd like to push . . ." '

'What's this then?' said Mrs Collinge. 'A get-well note?'

One way and another it was a relief to reach home that evening. Mum was upstairs when he arrived so he slipped into the new garden, very quietly, and fetched the coal shovel, equally quietly, and went down to the excavation.

Since the discovery of the thermostat on Saturday, nothing more had come up except a sash weight and a bicycle pedal. He was in two minds what to do with them. If he threw them away they would probably turn out to be valuable. Unless he showed them to Chris he wouldn't know if they were valuable or not. If he showed them to Chris, Chris might take them away.

Mum came out of the house and joined him.

'Who's been in trouble, then?' she asked.

Matthew wondered which of his troubles she was talking about. She had left school before the letter episode so she could mean either the football row or the history chart, which was a chronic complaint. He decided that she meant the history chart.

'Did Mrs Collinge tell you?'

'I didn't need to be told. What have you been doing?'

'That's what I haven't done,' said Matthew. 'I said I'd done something and I hadn't.'

'Well serve you right, then,' said Mum. 'Serve you right

for not doing it and serve you right for saying you'd done that when you hadn't. Now cheer up, she won't be cross for ever.'

'I haven't done that yet,' said Matthew.

'Oh, get along with you,' said Mum. 'Too busy digging holes, I suppose. You deserve whatever's coming to you.' She cuffed him gently and went indoors. It was a friendly cuff, but not so friendly as a kiss.

Dad was even less friendly about it. He suggested that whatever it was that Matthew hadn't done, he had better go upstairs right now, and do it.

And when was he going to mend his puncture?

16. Bottles

Jones the Bookrest was the eldest of Mrs Bagnall's cats. He was named after the people she had bought him from and he spent most of his time asleep in people's laps, so mountainous and immobile that you could prop a book against him and he wouldn't disturb it. At the moment he was lying on the path at the side of the house, watching Matthew trying to repair his puncture. Occasionally he would stretch out his neck and take an idle drink from the bowl of water that Matthew was using to test the inner tube for leaks.

In the distance Mrs Bagnall called her flock in to breakfast with high pitched cries of 'Meat! Meat! Meat!' Jones the Bookrest got up, very slowly, and waded through the grass to the hedge, his fur skirt trailing round his paws. Matthew followed him into the new garden because Jones was too infirm to climb over the wall without assistance. He picked him up, his hands sinking deep into the thick pile of Jones's coat, and lifted him over, lowering him gently onto the rockery that was built in the angle of the wall on the Bagnalls' side.

'Pathetic,' said Mr Bagnall, glaring through the bare boughs of his apple trees. 'Cats that have to be lifted over walls ought to be put out of their misery.'

'But he's not ill, is he?' asked Matthew. 'Only a bit stiff.'

'He'd be even stiffer if I had my way,' said Mr Bagnall

and drove Jones the Bookrest indoors, leaving Matthew to hope that he didn't mean what he thought he did.

He returned to the bowl of water. The inner tube lay across it, so like a dead eel that his fingers twitched when he bent to pick it up. It was not a dead eel, but it was certainly a dead inner tube and he threw it down again. There was no chance of using the bicycle now until he bought a new one.

He went upstairs to see how much money there was in the tobacco tin that he used for a money box. The coins rolled out, smelling of Golden Virginia, and fell in a very small heap on the bed.

He was saving up for Christmas presents, but when he saw how small the heap was he realized that if he bought the tube there would be about enough left over to treat his family to a liquorice bootlace each. He put the money back in the tin and resigned himself to the fact that there was a lot of walking to be done between now and Christmas.

He went for the eggs on foot.

The early morning shadow of the house stretched down the field and Charlie stood upon the chimney stacks with his shotgun. Yew ran up and down the furrows, pursuing game that no one but himself could see.

'Morning,' said Charlie, as Matthew went by. 'Met Sir Oliver yet?'

'No,' said Matthew. 'Have you?'

'I reckon the tractor frightened him off,' said Charlie. 'If anyone see him, that'll be Yew, and he don't say nothing.'

'You know that bit of stone in your fireplace,' said Matthew. 'Mr Bagnall told me about that. It's Sir Oliver's crest that he wore on his helmet. He built the priory.'

'He had a strong old neck, then,' said Charlie. 'That block must weigh about fifty pounds.'

When Matthew came back Charlie had gone although Yew was still roistering in the field. The Angels' lorry was in the loke but when Matthew came out of Mrs Harrison's garden it was disappearing down the Hoxenham road. He went into the new garden and found Paul was there before him, already digging. He had started a new hole nearer the oak tree and Clive was sitting on the back doorstep, watching Paul and growling softly.

'He's winning the R.A.C. Rally,' said Paul. 'Don't take any notice and he'll drive for hours.'

'What are you doing here?' asked Matthew. Paul's excavation was neatly marked out with string wound round pegs.

'Dad dropped us off on the way to Tokesby,' said Paul. 'He'll be back later on. I had to bring Clive with me; Chris is out too.'

Matthew wondered, not for the first time, why Clive didn't stay at home with his mother. Even at this early hour he looked as if he had been wearing his clothes all night, and his hair stood on end like brown grass.

'Is Chris here?' asked Matthew, looking round. There was no sign of anyone else, but the Angels had a habit of appearing suddenly, like partridges from a seemingly empty field.

'No, he's with Dad. They've got a rush job on,' said Paul. Matthew realized that he was going to be stuck with Paul all day.

'What are you going to do about food?' he asked, wondering if Paul had it in mind to pay them a visit towards lunch time.

'I made some sandwiches,' said Paul. 'But I had to hide the bag in case he started on them.' He nodded towards Clive who had stopped droning and was kicking away the loose mortar round the edge of the step.

'Won't he get bored?' asked Matthew. Clive never seemed to have any toys to play with. He broke into a frantic hee-hawing.

'Air horns,' said Paul. 'He'll be all right. Look, are you

116

going to dig in your own hole or do you want to help me with this one?'

Matthew had no desire to become Paul's assistant. 'I'll start a new one of my own,' he said. If he wasn't careful, the Angels would take over the excavation and there would be nothing left for him to do but stand back with an admiring smile while they dug up the priory and removed it, bit by bit.

The coal shovel was lying in the excavation where he had left it last night. He took it a little way down the garden, towards the wall, and drove it into the cropped grass. The turf lifted easily: he removed two or three slices and threw them aside. He could never get his turfs quite square and he wished he had thought of pegging out the area before Paul had done it. If he did it now it would look like copying and although he didn't see much wrong with copying, himself, he had discovered at school that very few people shared his opinion, especially the ones who were being copied. He didn't care very much what Paul thought of him; what Paul might say was another matter.

Clive grew tired of demolishing the step and wandered towards him.

'I dig.'

'Go and help Paul,' said Matthew. Clive approached his brother.

'I dig.'

'No,' said Paul. 'Go and drive your car.'

Clive didn't argue. He looked defeated and went back to the step where he sat stroking his own hand, comfortingly, and talking to himself.

'He's learning,' said Paul, to Matthew.

'Cheer up, darling,' said Clive, to Clive.

It was mid-afternoon when Paul made his discovery. He and Clive had eaten their sandwiches on the site while Matthew went home for lunch.

'Wouldn't they like to come in here?' Mum had asked.

'No,' lied Matthew. 'They're having a picnic.'

He was just returning when he heard the crunch of crushed glass and Paul shouting. He ran to see what had happened and found Paul on his knees in his excavation, holding Clive at arm's length with one hand and scrabbling in the earth with the other.

'Look at that,' said Paul. Matthew looked and looked again, trying to locate the source of the excitement. All he could see was a mud-encrusted heap of green glass. Paul had dug up a bottle and smashed it in the process.

'What a fantastic bottle,' said Matthew, trying to sound both interested and sarcastic, depending on whether Paul was serious or not.

'This one's nothing. It's a pity I smashed it, but I didn't realize it was there until I hit it. There's a lot more underneath,' said Paul. Matthew had a flashback of the bottles at the Bridewell museum and wished that he had spent more time in looking at them. He had at least expected to find bottles.

'Have you got a hearth brush?' asked Paul. 'We must do this properly; we can't afford to break any more.'

'You're getting tidy, all of a sudden,' said Matthew. 'You don't have to sweep up.'

'We have to proceed with great caution now,' said Paul. 'Some of these might be valuable, they look very old. Go and get that brush.'

Matthew fetched the brush from the living-room fireplace. He was leaving with it when he ran into Mum.

'Now where are you going with that?' she said, when she noticed him trying to conceal it under his coat. 'Is this more of your digging nonsense?'

Matthew explained about the bottles.

'Well, I've heard of some daft pastimes, but I suppose Paul knows what he's doing.' She let him take the brush.

Paul was using the trowel to scrape away the broken

glass. He took the brush and dusted the soil. More bottles began to appear, lying on their sides in orderly rows.

'It's a glass graveyard,' said Paul. 'Old bottles come here to die. Was your Mr Blakely a secret drinker?'

'Not very secret,' said Matthew. 'He used to go down to the Bull at Calstead every night.'

'That's closed now,' said Paul, still brushing.

'Yes. Dad said they closed soon after he moved. He reckoned they couldn't make that pay after he'd gone,' said Matthew.

'When did he come here?'

'About eleven years ago,' said Matthew. 'I can't remember him very well, but everyone else can. If anybody does anything extra daft they say, that's just the kind of thing old Batty Blakely would have done.'

'Eleven years,' said Paul. 'These bottles are older than that. More like a hundred years. I'm not sure, but they look like they've been blown. They must be old. Who lived here before Blakely?'

'I don't know,' said Matthew. 'These used to be tied cottages before old Mr Hemp sold them. All sorts of people lived here. That bit of car wasn't Mr Blakely's, either. I asked Dad and he said they'd never had a Morris 10. Can I have that back?'

Paul inserted the point of the trowel under the topmost bottle and lifted it out of the earth. It was as black as treacle.

'I'll wash it in your sink,' said Paul. 'Your Mum won't mind?'

'Not if you do it,' said Matthew, sourly. 'Anyway, she's gone shopping.'

'In that case I'll borrow the phone as well,' said Paul. 'If I may? Chris might be home by now. I'd like him to see these.'

'That's in the hall by the front door,' said Matthew. 'Where's Clive got to?' The doorstep was vacant.

Paul was too interested in the bottle to bother about Clive. He headed for the hole in the hedge.

'You know, this really is worth finding,' he said, as he vanished. 'He can't have gone far; his legs are too short.'

Matthew thought that Clive could get up a fair turn of speed when it suited him. He looked in the hole first, and then searched around Kingston Villa, but all the doors were locked. By now, Clive might be rioting round Myhill Street, causing damage for which Matthew would be blamed.

Or he might be run over.

Matthew hurried down the loke to the Hoxenham Road. It was empty in both directions, except for Mr Catchpole Senior's goat which was looking through his front gate. Matthew went to ask if the Bagnalls had seen Clive. Mr Bagnall was behind the hedge, breaking up clumps of Madonna lilies.

'Clive?' he said, when Matthew inquired. 'The little lad with the black eye? He came over the wall ten minutes ago, looking for cats. He's with Marge, indoors.'

Marge was Mrs Bagnall.

'He didn't have a black eye when I saw him last,' said Matthew, alarmed.

'Well, maybe it was dirt,' said Mr Bagnall. 'That child needs a good scrape with silver sand. Hey, get out of that, you horrible mog,' he roared, hurling a lily bulb at a passing cat.

'Can I go and fetch him?' said Matthew, anxious to get away. Mr Bagnall seemed to have forgotten their friendly chat in the vestry.

'Please do,' said Mr Bagnall. 'Remove him at once. Take the cats as well if you like. And Matthew,' he added, more gently, 'don't nag him.'

'I never nagged him,' said Matthew and knocked at the back door. Mrs Bagnall answered it.

'Looking for Clive?' she said. 'He's in the living-room,

with the cats. Isn't he a bit young to be wandering about on his own?'

'They let him do as he likes,' said Matthew. 'He's such a pest I think they're quite glad when he does go away.'

Clive was sitting beside a big fur rug in front of the fire. A live coal rolled across the hearth and the whole rug swelled sideways.

It was the cats.

The rug was deep and soft in the middle, where lay Furbelow and Jones the Bookrest, lumpy at one end, which was pregnant Minnie, and ragged at the other, where Tokyo Rose and Genghis Khan reclined on their elbows and swatted at each other with limp paws. Supercat was in the garden, annoying Mr Bagnall.

Clive stared with round eyes and both hands in his mouth. Then he swooped, arms spread wide, and the rug ran away in several directions. He was left clasping Minnie.

'Don't squeeze her,' said Mrs Bagnall, trying to free the cat. 'She's going to have kittens.'

'Ought to be shot,' said Mr Bagnall, coming in with a basket of lily bulbs. 'You can give these to your mother,' he said, handing Matthew the basket.

'Kittings,' said Clive. 'I have.'

'We'd better go home now,' said Matthew. 'Your Dad might come and wonder where you are.' He put his hand on Clive's shoulder. Clive made himself very small and heavy. He wrapped his arms more tightly round Minnie.

'I stay,' he said.

'You can come and see her again,' said Mrs Bagnall, 'but you must let her go now. You'll hurt her.' Minnie struggled and wailed.

'Singing cat,' said Clive, blandly.

Mr Bagnall stepped in. 'Put her down at once, Clive,' he said. Clive obeyed.

'Thank you,' said Mr Bagnall. 'Now you're going home with Matthew. Yes?'

'Yes,' said Clive. Matthew dragged him out of the bunga-low towards the gate.

Mr Catchpole's goat smiled at them from across the road.

'Dog,' said Clive, attempting to visit it.

'Goat. Goats bite,' said Matthew, untruthfully, for it was an elderly nanny goat with a coy nature.

The new garden was empty and so was the old.

'All gone,' said Clive, looking under a flower pot. Matthew heard a tapping sound above them. Paul was in Matthew's bedroom, knocking on the window.

'What are you doing up there?' Matthew shouted, and ran to find out, tucking Clive under his arm to save time. Paul came out of the bedroom as they reached the top of the stairs.

'There was no one in when I rang,' he explained, 'so I thought I'd look round. What's that you've got on your window sill?'

Matthew set Clive on his feet. 'Stick insects,' he said. 'Who asked you to go into my room?'

'I thought they might be,' said Paul. 'But I couldn't see them.' He went back to the bedroom, still uninvited, for another look.

'Oh yes, there they are. What are they for?'

'They're not for anything,' said Matthew. 'They're my pets.'

'Yes,' said Paul, looking at him out of the tail of his eye. 'They would be. Most exciting pets in the world, after house bricks.'

'What have you got, rats?' asked Matthew.

'Anything worth watching on telly?' said Paul, leading the way downstairs to the living-room. 'Is it a colour set?' He switched it on.

'We can't afford colour,' said Matthew. 'But we get foreign stations. We can get the news in German and motor racing from Holland, but we don't get any sound with that.'

The set warmed up and a painful pattern of zig-zags buzzed up and down the screen.

'Makes your eyeballs click, doesn't it?' said Paul, taking liberties with switches that Matthew was not allowed to touch. 'Not much point in getting German news if you want to watch Match of the Day, is it?' He made another adjustment. 'How about University Challenge with Belgian subtitles? Oh look, there's that fellow who plays the brain surgeon in wotsitsname.'

'I don't watch that,' said Matthew. 'University Challenge isn't on today. Why don't you let that alone? You'll break something.'

'No I won't,' said Paul. 'What's this?'

'That's our barometer.'

'Why's it all done up like a cuckoo clock?'

'My Gran bought that in Margate.' Paul began to un-hook it. 'Leave that alone!'

Paul was so surprised to hear Matthew snap that he did leave it alone. His eyes orbited the room, looking for new prey. Matthew heard a vehicle on the loke and looked out of the window.

'Here's your Dad,' he said, with relief. Paul went out and Matthew heard him undoing all the bolts on the front door. Clive followed him, then he changed his mind and stood in the doorway, waving politely to Matthew.

'I go,' he said.

Matthew watched round the curtain until the lorry reached the end of the loke. Then he ran to the new garden. Paul's excavation was covered with a sheet of corrugated iron with 'Do not remove' chalked offensively across it.

Matthew considered this advice for a moment, and then lifted the iron. The bottles were his for the taking. How pleasant it would be to lift them all, now, and leave an empty grave for the Angels to find tomorrow.

How very unpleasant, on the other hand, to lift them all and break them, which was almost certainly what would happen. He put the corrugated iron back again, making sure that it was in exactly the right place, and wrote a rude word under 'Do not remove'. Then he rubbed it out again because it wasn't quite rude enough for Paul, and far too rude for Mum, who might see it first, by mistake. And he wasn't sure that he had spelled it right.

17. No Bottles

Matthew walked round the garden, enjoying the loneliness, and making grey footprints in the frost until he was disturbed by the sound of a car, and Mr Angel's Volvo drew up at the gate. Chris was driving with Paul beside him and Julie and Karen holding down Clive at the back.

As Paul got out of the car, Matthew saw that he was empty handed.

'Where's our bottle?' he demanded. Paul shrugged.

'I left it at home. It'll be safer there.'

'That would be safer here,' said Matthew. He had felt misgivings last night when he saw Paul bear the bottle away, cradling it in his arms, while Clive trundled backwards behind him, dragging the bag that had contained their sandwiches. Now he might never get it back.

Chris nodded to him and strode into the back garden, followed by Paul, then Julie, then Karen. Clive went last, as he always did, and Matthew was about to follow, but he refused to bring up the rear, inferior even to Clive. He waited till they were out of sight and then ran round to his own garden, so that he was approaching from his own territory. None of the Angels seemed to notice, but he felt he was making a point, if only to himself.

Chris removed the sheet of corrugated iron and propped it against the wall. On top of the bottles lay a dead starling. Chris flicked it aside.

'Who put that there?'

'I didn't,' said Matthew. 'I expect one of the cats caught that and it escaped and died of wounds. They won't eat starlings.'

'Go and bury it, Karen,' said Paul. 'You can have a little funeral.'

'Don't touch it,' said Julie. 'Birds have fleas.' Clive picked it up by the tail to stroke it and Julie slapped it out of his hand. 'You get rid of it, Matthew.'

'Why should I? I don't want fleas.'

'I don't mind fleas,' said Chris, taking the starling and throwing it over the wall. 'But they're so difficult to catch.'

'I spit on them,' said Paul. 'They can't jump when they're wet.'

Julie's eyes became pieces of cold green soap.

'That's disgusting,' she said. She took Karen by the arm and pulled her away. Clive went after them and Chris availed himself of the extra room. He took up the trowel and began to scrape away the earth. As each bottle came loose, Paul picked it up and laid it on the grass. Matthew started to pick one up.

'Don't do that,' said Chris. 'They must be handled very gently.'

'I'm not going to break it,' said Matthew, and picked up the bottle anyway. Paul took it from him and put it back in the grass.

'Wait till they're all up,' he said. 'Then we'll take them home and wash them.'

'No. We'll wash them here,' said Matthew, certain that once the bottles left the premises they would never come back. He picked it up again. 'I'll wash this one now.'

'Put it down,' said Chris. 'Don't fight over it.' Matthew considered crowning him with the bottle. Instead he turned away, still holding it. Paul came after him.

'Chris said to put it down.'

'Why should I do what he says?'

'But he knows all about these things. Those bottles are

real antiques. That's why I waited till today to get them out.' Paul trotted beside him, his head on one side, like Yew after favours.

'I know,' said Matthew. 'I'm not that thick. I could have got them out myself, couldn't I? After you'd gone. But I'm going to share them now.'

'Of course,' said Paul. 'So put it back.'

'I'm going to wash it, that's all. I want to see what that looks like.'

'It looks just like the one we found yesterday,' said Paul. 'You can see that without washing it.'

'Yes,' said Matthew. 'But I never saw the one we found yesterday. You took it away before I saw that clean.' He managed to get into the kitchen ahead of Paul, and started to fill the sink with warm water. 'Why haven't you brought that back?'

He lowered the bottle into the sink. Paul put his hand on it, intending to take it back. When he saw that Matthew wasn't going to let go he went on holding it, to imply that the bottle was safe only under his supervision.

Matthew stirred the water with his free hand, sending quite a lot of it up Paul's sleeve, by accident. He wanted to reach for the scrubbing brush, but he dared not let go of the bottle while Paul was touching it.

Mum came into the kitchen with a bag of potatoes.

'Now what are you two doing in the sink?' she said. 'Stand aside, I want to clean these potatoes now.'

Paul and Matthew stood aside, still hanging on to the bottle. Mum looked at the dirty water in the sink.

'What on earth are you up to?' she asked and without waiting for an answer she plunged her arm into the sink, seized the bottle and whipped it out of the water before either of them could get a good grip on it. A stream of muddy liquid, water and other things, poured out of the bottle and hit the draining board, splashing up against the wall behind the sink.

Mum turned the bottle upside down, shook it to make sure that it was empty, and put it on the high shelf above the cooker.

'If you want to wash dirt you can do that in a bucket in the garden,' she said. She drove them outside and shut the door. Matthew didn't argue. At least the bottle was safe from the Angels for a time.

'You make trouble,' said Paul. 'I told you not to wash it here.'

'You don't tell me anything,' said Matthew, but quietly so that Paul should not hear. Paul was one of many. Matthew was one alone.

'Pest,' said Chris. 'Pain in the neck.' Matthew stayed at the other end of the garden after that, while he and Paul dug up the rest of the bottles. He looked into the original hole and found it occupied. Across the top was the piece of iron with 'Do not remove' on it. Ignoring the instruction he lifted the corner to see what was going on below and found Julie, Karen, and Clive installed with dolls and biscuits.

'Go away,' said Karen. 'This is our house now.'

'That's not your house, that's my hole,' said Matthew.

'Well, we've got that now,' said Julie. 'Paul said you weren't using that anymore. He said you were digging another hole. He said you'd go on digging holes till your head fell off if nobody stopped you.'

Matthew moved the roof to one side and they sat there, blinking palely at him, like a nest of night-loving animals surprised by the sun. The hole had changed since he last looked in it. There was a newspaper carpet on the floor, an upturned seed box to act as a table, a flower pot full of earth with dead Michaelmas daisies stuck in it. At one side stood a broken step ladder for getting in and out.

Clive was sitting on the bottom step of the ladder. He was not permitted to join the party on the carpet.

'When did you do all this?'

'Just now,' said Julie. 'While you were mobbing Paul. See, you didn't even know we were doing it. That's ours now. Put the roof back. Go away.'

'I wasn't mobbing Paul,' said Matthew.

'Go away.'

He went. Mum had left the kitchen so he sneaked indoors. The sink was drained and the potatoes were bubbling on the stove. He looked up at the shelf above it, intending to repossess the bottle, but the shelf was empty. He could hear the vacuum cleaner in the living-room and stormed in there to find Mum.

'What's happened to the bottle?' he said, but he was down wind of the vacuum cleaner. Mum turned to face him, her hand cupped to her ear.

'What happened to the bottle?'

'What happened to what?' said Mum, shaking her head to show that she still couldn't hear him.

'What happened to the bottle?' shouted Matthew. The steaming rage that had sent him out of the kitchen was beginning to lose pressure. He stamped on the button at the end of the cleaner and the wheezing died away. 'The bottle,' he repeated. 'Who took it?'

'You're in a mind,' said Mum. 'Don't take it out on the Hoover.' She pulled it out of his reach. 'Chris came in and asked for it so I gave it to him.'

'You shouldn't have,' said Matthew. 'They won't give that back.'

'Don't shout,' said Mum. 'If he wants to collect dirty bottles, why shouldn't he? Though I'd have thought he'd have something better to do at his age.'

'Those bottles are ours. They were dug up in our garden.'

'Yes, but we don't want them, do we?' said Mum, who could never see that her ideas about dirt were not shared by Matthew.

'I want them,' he said. 'They're the first properly historic things we've dug up and they won't let me touch them.'

'Who dug them up?'

'Paul did,' said Matthew, 'but that was my idea. If he hadn't seen me digging in the first place he'd never have thought of it. He didn't know there was anything to dig for when he first came. He didn't know he was going to find bottles and now they won't let me have even one. They're taking them all. They're taking everything.'

'Do you want me to ask for it back?' said Mum, knowing quite well that he didn't.

'No,' said Matthew. 'They'd talk you out of it. They can get round you.'

This was the wrong answer and Mum switched on the Hoover again, to show that the conversation was at an end.

18. Teeth

The day of the school photograph was a moveable feast, but it usually fell in November, in plenty of time for Christmas, so that grannies and aunties could be given the portraits as Christmas presents. On Monday Mr Postle arrived, hung about with cameras, and lessons were abandoned while the rooms were rearranged for the photographs. Miss Cooper and the infants moved into the junior room, and the juniors were all squeezed up together at the end tables to make room for them, while Mr Postle set up his equipment on the other side of the partition. Then they went in, one after the other, to smile at the camera.

Mr Postle had odd ideas about making people smile. He liked to see plenty of teeth and only little ones, with gaps at the front, were allowed to smile with their mouths shut. Matthew liked Mr Postle, but hated to be photographed with his mouth open because it made him look barmy.

'Mum says she wants me to look normal,' he said, when it was his turn.

'So you do,' said Mr Postle, cheerfully. 'Dead normal.' Then he added, as he always did, 'Open wide, let's see all those teeth.'

'You should have been a dentist,' said Matthew, soundlessly, between clenched jaws.

'You look like a terrier with a rat,' said Mr Postle, sighing. They had this argument every time. 'O.K. Close your mouth; but at least look happy. Your Mum wants you to look happy, doesn't she?'

Matthew was not feeling happy. He still had his row with the Angels to think about and in the other room Mrs Collinge was looking at the history charts. All the charts but his own were finished and some people, those with large handwriting, had started a second. One of these was Roger Howlett. His charts hung on either side of Matthew's, making it look emptier than ever.

Mr Postle looked out of the window.

'Here comes the vicar on his religious-type motor bike,' he said. 'He won't start praying, will he? I've got nine more to do, yet.'

'He's going to be in the big photo with all of us,' said Matthew. 'Can I go now?'

'I suppose so,' said Mr Postle. 'I can't do anything more for you. Why don't you practise smiling?'

Matthew produced a horrid smirk and went through the partition to fetch Peter who was next in line for a photograph. He had just arrived at school, an hour late.

'Open wide,' said Matthew as he passed Peter in the doorway. Peter shook his head.

'I've got a gap, now,' he said, displaying it. All his top front teeth had gone, leaving a fang at each side. 'I got them kicked out on Friday at Clipton. I've just been down the clinic. My Mum, she didn't half howl when she saw that.'

'Didn't you howl?' asked Matthew, feeling the kick himself.

'Not much, but that do make you spit,' said Peter, retreating in a cloud of fine spray.

The vicar, his crash helmet under his arm, was admiring the history charts with Mrs Collinge. Matthew sidled out to fetch the milk for break, but they were waiting for him when he got back.

'Matthew's having a bit of trouble with his, aren't you, Matthew?' said Mrs Collinge. Matthew inferred that there was more trouble to come. He looked at his feet and waited to see if the vicar would say anything before it was his turn to speak.

'It seems very promising,' said the vicar, looking round, uncertainly, for he didn't know which of the charts they were talking about.

'Very promising,' said Mrs Collinge. 'All promises and nothing else, so far. Did you do anything over the weekend?'

Matthew tried rapidly to edit the events of the last two days so that he could say something that was both true and would satisfy Mrs Collinge.

At last he said, 'I found some bottles in the garden. They were very old.'

He had forgotten about Julie. She bounced out of her seat, tightly plaited and frilled for the photograph, and pushed past him.

'Miss, that's not true. My cousin Paul found the bottles and Matthew tried to take them away from him.'

'That's not true either,' said Matthew. 'Paul took them away from me.'

'Paul found them.'

'He found them in my garden.'

'It seems to me,' said Mrs Collinge, 'that neither of you knows what the truth is. You'd better go away and decide what really happened, and don't tell tales,' she called after Julie, not a moment too soon for Matthew's liking.

He waited for Julie to stop and argue and give his secret away. It would be better to tell Mrs Collinge himself than to have it come out in that false fashion, but as soon as he started to speak Mrs Collinge said, 'Matthew, don't talk about it, for Heaven's sake. Go and do something.'

Sooner or later he would have to admit that he hadn't done anything for the chart and all his secrets about Sir Oliver and the priory would be exposed to ridicule and contempt. He would have to admit that he had been digging a hole instead of doing his homework: that the pictures he had been drawing to keep Mum happy were rubbish. It was too much to think about all at once. He sat down at his work but his mind was weak with despair. It was too late to do anything now and the charts were supposed to be finished on Friday. He would stop being Head Boy on Friday. The world ended on Friday.

Julie read his thoughts.

'Darren will be back this time next week. You won't be Head Boy any more. That's a good thing. You're a liar.'

'I'll kill you. I'll wring your neck, kkkkkkh!' said Matthew, but not out loud. He couldn't sit at the table with Julie's venomous hissing in his ear and there was really no room to work until Mr Postle left, so he went to the back of the class and made a discreet show of tidying the museum.

The prize exhibit was the Catchpole axe. Hardly anything matched that for impressiveness because it was so untouchably old. Roger had brought some pieces of stained glass from the Old Hall and Anne Lilley had loaned a brass bedknob that had to go back on the bed at the end of term, but many of the things did not properly belong in the museum at all, such as the dried bracket fungus, the wrens' nest and the grebe's feet. Matthew had argued for a long time with Trevor Lilley, who owned the feet, but Trevor insisted that they ought to be on show because they were old, which was certainly true. They were practically mummified and stood with stiff pride in the middle of the table.

When it was time for the big photograph they all went into the playground with Mr Postle. Mrs Sadler and Mrs Howlett arrived in their best coats and Mum came out of the kitchen to sit in the middle of the picture with Mrs Collinge, Miss Cooper and the vicar.

'Hurry up,' said Mr Postle. 'This isn't the weather for sitting out of doors.'

It was a bright day, and cold. Matthew and Peter brought out the long benches from the cloakroom.

'I'm a vampire,' said Peter, fangs glistening. 'I saw the

dentist and he's going to make me false teeth like Grandad's got.'

'Not a whole set?' said Matthew.

'No, just some front ones with a little pink thing like a crab at the back,' said Peter. 'I can take that out and frighten the girls.'

A cobweb of mist lay round Myhill Street, held there by the trees. As Matthew walked up the footpath Mr Angel floated into sight, sitting on the roof like Noah adrift on his ark.

'Almost finished,' called Mr Angel, when Matthew was within earshot. The house wore its new roof with a jaunty air and the chimney, which Mr Angel was repointing, stuck up like a feather in its cap.

'Won't you be coming back any more?' asked Matthew, with a sudden rush of hope to his head.

'No,' said Mr Angel. 'Not till Saturday. Got to get on with the inside after this.'

'Oh.' For a happy moment Matthew had thought he had seen the last of the Angels.

'I reckon we'll be in and out till Christmas.' Mr Angel began to reverse down the ladder. 'Is your Mum about?'

'She's delivering parish magazines with Mrs Sadler,' said Matthew. 'Can I give her a message?'

'Just tell her what I told you,' said Mr Angel. 'Got to pick up Clive from his auntie's.' He wiped his dirty hands on his dirtier overall and began to leave. Matthew had an idea and stopped him.

'Can I have my bottles back, please?'

'Bottles? What bottles? I haven't got any bottles,' said Mr Angel. 'What are you talking about?'

'Paul borrowed a few bottles belonging to me,' said Matthew. 'I need to have them back.' That was true enough. The bottles were his only hope on Friday.

'Well, you'd better ask him,' said Mr Angel. 'Ring him up.'

That would be no good. Paul would escape too easily. No one ever went to war on a telephone.

'When does he get home from school?'

Mr Angel was in a hurry to leave and he walked backwards, Matthew trailing him.

'What's today, Wednesday? He stay late on Wednesdays. Try him tomorrow about half past four.'

He climbed into his cab and the lorry skidded down the loke, flints cracking out from under the wheels.

'I'm going over to Hoxenham tomorrow, after school,' said Matthew, when Mum came home.

'Have you mended your puncture, then?'

'No, I'll get the bus at the church,' said Matthew. 'There's one goes by soon after we come out.'

'You ought to mend that.'

'I need a new inner tube,' said Matthew. 'I can't afford a new one until after Christmas.'

'Well, don't ask Dad for that,' said Mum. 'He's always telling you to walk down the loke. You never listen to what people tell you. Since you got to be Head Boy you've become sillier and sillier.'

'I won't be Head Boy after Monday,' said Matthew. 'Darren's coming back.'

'Did you ever write to him?'

'I forgot.'

'Why don't you go and see him?'

'I don't know.' Darren had become faint and foreign since he went away. Matthew had nothing to say to him and when Darren found out what he had been doing he would have nothing to say to Matthew. Darren's idea of a good time did not include digging holes.

19. Armageddon

'When are you going to get your chart done, then?' said Peter, closing the gate. 'That's got to be finished tomorrow.'

'I've got some things on loose paper,' said Matthew. 'I'll stick them on in the morning.'

Friday was waiting for him like a burning fiery furnace and there was no way of avoiding it unless he died tonight. All that concerned him was the number of lies he had to tell between now and tomorrow morning. After that he could stop lying, stop pretending and stop digging. The Christmas pudding had failed him and he had found nothing. At this moment it seemed quite crazy that he had ever expected to, and yet he had believed for so long, and his faith had failed him because all the time he was digging he had been sure that Sir Oliver had wanted him to find something too, to ease his lonely ghost as it walked on the causeway.

'Mrs Collinge will kill you,' said Peter, cheerfully. 'You've gone all to pieces this term.' As a First Division manager in the making he had to practise being ruthless. He made a sprightly leap onto his bicycle and sailed off down the Calstead Road, while Matthew walked to the bus stop.

Officially it was by the church gate but the road was so narrow that it was safest to wait by the dell until the bus came into sight, down at Iken's Fen. The sycamore leaves had fallen at last and the gas stoves were white in the blue shadows. Matthew looked down, and suddenly realized what they reminded him of.

Stonehenge.

Stovehenge.

It was a pun, like the owl and Sir Oliver, only it was a much better pun and his own invention. Matthew took a few minutes off from his private worries to feel pleased with himself.

Mrs Bagnall was driving towards him and she stopped when she saw who was standing there.

'You're not watching those wretched stoves again, are you,' she said. 'What do you expect them to do; get up and dance?'

'Stovehenge,' said Matthew, and Mrs Bagnall laughed. She was still smiling as she drove away. Matthew stared after her. For the first time in his life he had made somebody laugh on purpose, and it hadn't been difficult. He might be able to do it again.

When the bus came he sat well away from all the people who might talk to him and rehearsed what he was going to say when he met Paul. He hoped there wouldn't be a fight. Paul was bigger and the Angels' resemblance to Stone Age man wasn't wholly facial. Matthew hadn't fought anyone since the day he caught Roger Howlett testing a new pen knife on his Wellington boots, and they had both been infants then.

Hoxenham was empty when he got off the bus at the staithe. The boats and the ducks had the broad to themselves and the seagulls cruising overhead were tinted pink underneath by the low-lying sun.

He had an hour to accomplish his mission before the last bus left for Pallingham so he set off for the Angel estate, a long way from the bus stop.

The garden was as silent as the broad. The wrecked vehicles loomed in the cold air and there was no one about. Matthew looked first into the garage but the inspection pit was bare and Chris's car had gone. Fat Sally, now missing all her wheels, stood forlorn in the corner.

He knocked at the bathroom door and tried the handle but it was locked and no one came. He walked all round the house. The windows were blind and when he pressed the bell at what would have been the front door, if the house had had a front, it rang in the hollow, deserted way that bells do, in an empty house.

He had forgotten that all the Angels might be out; they didn't know he was coming. He was about to leave when he heard footsteps on the road. He withdrew into the shadow of the garage and watched the gateway where the willow tree stood with its notice. Geo. Angel. Builder and decorator. Paul walked round the tree and began to stroll up the drive. Matthew was glad to see that he was alone. He thought he could deal with Paul if Paul had no one to reinforce him. He stepped out of the garage and propped himself against the wall of the bathroom so that Paul wouldn't see him until he turned the corner. The footsteps paused as Paul stopped by the garage. Matthew could imagine him standing there, ears pricked, sniffing the air, conscious that strangers were in the area.

He looked round the corner and said 'Hello.'

Paul jumped slightly and smiled. Matthew was almost inclined to forget about the bottles but he had a dark suspicion that Paul knew why he had come.

'Have you been here long?' asked Paul. 'Our school bus was late.'

'Not long,' said Matthew. 'I came by bus too.'

'All this way on a bus, just to see me?' said Paul and he made the smile stretch even further.

'I came to see how the bottles were getting along,' said Matthew.

'All this way just to see the bottles?'

'I'd like to have a look at them,' said Matthew. 'I haven't really seen them yet. And I need one for school.'

'They're quite safe,' said Paul, still smiling, with something in the smile that was intended to remind Matthew that the bottles were behind locked doors and Matthew was outside. He made no move to go in.

'Well, can I see them?' said Matthew. 'I must have one.' The lines round Paul's smile vanished and a new set appeared on his forehead. Suddenly he was frowning.

'I don't know if I ought to get them out. Chris isn't here,' he said, his eyes sliding about under the frown. He and Matthew both knew that Chris had nothing to do with it. It was merely a matter of waiting to see which of them gave in first. Paul had finished his piece. It was Matthew's turn.

'They aren't Chris's bottles,' he said. 'And they're mine as much as yours. Why shouldn't I see them?'

He stopped to see if Paul would refuse outright or think of a better excuse.

'We could have a quick look at them,' said Paul, suggesting that he was as helpless as Matthew over the fate of the bottles. Matthew stared him out.

'Go on then.'

'We mustn't touch them.' Perhaps he could grab one and run.

Paul produced a key and unlocked the bathroom door. Matthew crowded in behind him in case Paul swung round and locked him out. The bathroom had been transformed. There were three distinct rows of fingerprints round the walls, at diminishing heights, from Chris down to Clive. The bath was encircled by a whiskery tide mark and the carpet was crossed by three divergent paths; from door to door, from door to bath and from door to lavatory.

'What's happened?' asked Matthew, gazing about him with a brilliant memory of his first sight of the bathroom.

Paul seemed surprised. 'We've just been using it.'

They went through the living-room to the kitchen. 'Care for a drink?' said Paul as if he were about to produce brandy and cigars. He reached for the kettle.

'Just the bottles,' said Matthew. Paul hesitated, seeking further delaying tactics, and then shot out of the door so fast that Matthew had no time to see where he was going, and he was back before he had a chance to look out of the door himself. Paul was carrying one bottle, a poor relation of all the other bottles, with a wry neck and a cracked lip.

'I don't suppose Chris would mind too much if you kept this one,' he said, generously.

'Where are the rest?' asked Matthew, turning the bottle about so that they could both see how decrepit it was. Paul's eyes began to swivel again.

'Chris locked them up. I can't get at them,' he explained. 'We were afraid that Clive would break them.'

'I told you to leave them with me,' said Matthew. 'Clive wouldn't have got them at ours. I must have one for school – I shall get into a terrible row tomorrow if I haven't got anything.'

'You have got one,' said Paul.

'I don't want this horrible old thing, that's broken.'

'They're all like that.'

Matthew gaped at him. 'I thought I was supposed to be the liar,' he said. 'You think you can have anything you want. What's so special about you?'

He thought it was time for Paul to thump him and he put the bottle on the kitchen table, so as to be ready. Paul shook his head, gleaming with satisfaction because he could keep his temper and Matthew was losing his.

'You only want them because we've got them,' he said, in a voice calculated to hasten the process.

'They're out of our garden,' said Matthew. 'If you hadn't started digging it up all over the place, I'd have found them.'

'Oh yes,' said Paul. 'And what would you have done with them? You'd have chucked them away, wouldn't you? You think everything's rubbish unless it shines.'

He took a step forward and Matthew, thinking that this time Paul really was going to hit him, took a step back. His hip caught against the corner of the table and the two legs nearest to him were jolted clear of the ground. The bottle tipped, shuddered, and began to jig down the sloping table top. When it reached the edge it spun on its rim, stood for a second poised exquisitely on nothing, and then the virtue went out of it and it dropped to the floor.

All this seemed to take a very long time but it still happened too fast for them to stop the bottle. Matthew thought that Paul made no effort to move anyway.

When he could bear to look at him again the smile was back in place.

'Whose fault was that, then?' said Paul.

Matthew stared at the bottle. The neck lay where it had fallen, still intact and surrounded by black glass stars, dashed to the furthest corners of the kitchen.

'You can't have another one,' said Paul. 'It wouldn't be safe. What a good thing we didn't leave the rest with you. They'd all be like that, by now. Aren't you going to clear it up?'

Matthew walked towards the door.

'I'm not clearing that up,' he said. 'Get your mother to help you. You do what you like in my house. I'll do what I like in yours.'

Paul watched him, his fist in front of his mouth. Matthew understood that after saying nothing for so long he had now said too much.

'Get out,' said Paul.

'Go on, get your mother to clean it up,' shouted Matthew. 'No wonder she's never here. She must be as sick of you as I am.'

Paul's voice rose to an ugly scream.

'Get out! Get out! Get out!'

He was in the blackest disgrace and the blank history chart shone down on him like an accusing spotlight. When Mrs Collinge had finished telling him, in front of everyone, exactly what she thought of his work, or rather the lack of it, he was left to contemplate his sins while the others went out to play. He sat at the empty table: Mrs Collinge sat at her desk with a cup of tea, and looked at him from time to time. From time to time Matthew looked at Mrs Collinge and at last they both looked up at the same moment.

'Why did you lie about it?' said Mrs Collinge. 'I can't understand why you lied. You don't need me to tell you it was wrong, but it was so silly as well. You've done nothing at all for a whole month. You must have known I'd find out.'

'I was doing something,' said Matthew. 'But that's all gone wrong.'

'Well let me see it, even if it has gone wrong. At least I'll know you've tried.'

'That's at home.'

'Bring it in then. I want to see it,' said Mrs Collinge.

'I can't,' said Matthew. 'I really can't.'

'Then I can't believe you,' said Mrs Collinge. 'And I think I'd better speak to your mother about it.'

Matthew's resistance gave way.

'That's a hole,' he said. 'I dug a hole in the garden. When I said I was doing something, that's what it was.'

Mrs Collinge gave way too. She bowed her head low over the table.

'You mean you've been digging a hole in the garden for four weeks and calling it your homework?'

'That was work,' said Matthew. 'That was hard. I thought I was going to find something historic. There's a priory under our garden.'

'The priory would have been interesting – if you'd written about it instead of digging for it,' said Mrs Collinge. 'Did you honestly imagine you'd find anything by digging a hole?'

'I found out about Sir Oliver,' Matthew began. It was a mistake to mention Sir Oliver.

'I told you right at the beginning that we weren't interested in ghost stories,' said Mrs Collinge.

'He's not just a story. He really lived. He was famous, once,' cried Matthew. 'He was a verray parfit gentil knight.'

'I dare say,' said Mrs Collinge. 'But he hasn't done much for you, has he? And you haven't done much for him.' She looked pleased, for a moment. 'Do you know where that quotation comes from?'

'What quotation?'

'About the parfit gentil knight?'

'I didn't know that was a quotation,' said Matthew. 'I don't even know what it means.'

'Take the bottles away,' said Mrs Collinge.

When the rest of the class came back he crept outside with the milk bottles and parked them by the door. It was the last time he would do it; Darren took over again on Monday. Fortunately the row had taken place before Mum arrived. He looked over the fence to see if she was coming, but the mist hung low over Fen Street, and he could see nothing.

He was going to see quite enough of Mum later on.

'That's final then,' said Mum. 'No more digging. No more holes. No more lies. In future you come straight home and get on with your work.'

'What about when there isn't any work?' said Matthew.

'Let's get this straight,' said Dad, very weary. 'There's to be no more of this nonsense at all. You are not to go into that garden again until we cultivate it.'

'Yes,' said Matthew. 'Not even to talk to Mrs Bagnall? She might call me, or something. Or Mrs Harrison. I have to stand near her.'

'Stop looking for excuses,' said Mum. 'You are not to play in the garden any more.'

'It wasn't a game,' said Matthew. 'That wasn't playing. I only pretended it was so I could keep it a secret. I really did think I'd find something. And what about the Angels?' he demanded. 'I suppose they can go there when they like.'

'I'm not worried about the Angels,' said Dad. 'I'm worried about you. Very worried.'

'That means they can. Can't I just go over there and tidy up? I left some tools out when you called me in.'

'Hurry up, then,' said Dad. He reached for the Friday teacup, cooling beside him.

Matthew went into the garden and looked at it, seeing the excavation at last for what it was.

Nonsense.

He put the coal shovel away and tidied all the rubbish that he had dug up. There was only one place to put it, back in the hole. As he was leaving Mrs Bagnall came out on her step and began calling. 'Meat! Meat! Meat!' The cats pushed past her into the kitchen. Mrs Bagnall looked worried and called again. 'Minniminniminni.'

'Have you seen our Minnie?' she asked, noticing Matthew. 'She hasn't been home since last night.'

Matthew hadn't been paying much attention to the cats, lately. He tried to recall whether he had seen Minnie or not.

'I don't think so,' he said. 'Perhaps she's having her kittens.'

'I hope not,' said Mrs Bagnall. 'They're due any day and I want her at home. It's her first litter.'

'I'll bring her round if I see her,' said Matthew.

'You do that,' said Mrs Bagnall, and walked among the apple trees, calling again.

'Minniminniminnimin!'

20. Under the Autumn Garden

'Found any owls yet?' asked Charlie as Matthew went by on his way to collect the eggs.

'No,' said Matthew. Now that he was finished with the excavation everyone would keep talking about it.

'Seen Sir Oliver?'

'No.'

'You'd better hurry up,' said Charlie. 'That's his last night tonight. First of December tomorrow.'

It didn't matter any more.

Mr Bagnall, fierce and bristly in a dressing-gown, was snuffing fresh air at the back door when Matthew returned with the eggs. Beside him sat Jones the Bookrest, so immersed in fur that Matthew couldn't tell which end his head was.

'I don't think he knows which end his head is,' said Mr Bagnall, taking the eggs. 'The Living Blob. I suppose he is still alive,' he murmured, nudging Jones with his slipper. Jones allowed one eye to drop open for an instant.

'Still functioning,' said Mr Bagnall. 'I believe that there are certain organisms that can live for days after their brains have been removed.'

'Has Minnie come home yet?' asked Matthew and waited for Mr Bagnall to make an unkind remark.

All he said was, 'I'm afraid she hasn't. Keep an eye open for her, won't you? She's Marge's favourite.'

When Matthew reached the gate he turned to wave and

saw Mr Bagnall tickling Jones under the chin. He was beginning to form a theory about Mr Bagnall and the cats.

He rounded the corner into Ship Loke and the Angels were there already. He started to go into the garden of Kingston Villa, then recalled that it was forbidden and walked on to his own gate. Chris was removing a window frame in the front bedroom. He saw Matthew pass, but he didn't wave.

Clive and the girls were in Matthew's garden, hanging round the kitchen door.

'Go on over your own side,' said Matthew. 'You've got that all to yourselves. You don't need to come here.'

'You're not digging any more,' said Julie. 'I know why.'

'No you don't,' said Matthew. 'Where's Paul?'

'He didn't want to come,' said Julie. 'He says he's had enough of you.'

Karen said, 'Clive's eating something.'

'That's not chewing gum, is it?' asked Matthew, glancing towards Mum, in the kitchen. Clive might go indoors and park his gum in a tactless place. He put out his tongue. Coiled upon it was a red, elastic band.

Julie tried to take it, but Clive retracted his tongue and clamped his mouth shut.

'That'll get round your heart,' said Julie, balked. 'If you swallow that it will wind itself round your heart and choke you. You'll die.'

Clive chewed loudly.

'Don't be daft,' said Matthew. 'How could that get anywhere near his heart? What you swallow goes down a tube to your guts.'

'Guts is rude,' said Julie, turning her back. 'Come on, Karen, let's go and sit in our house.'

They ran to the gap in the hedge and Matthew went into the kitchen. Left alone, Clive sat down on the step and started the motor, his jaws working springily as the rubber band went round and round.

Julie's complaining face looked in at the door.

'Someone's left rubbish in our house.'

'I did,' said Matthew. 'I was clearing up. I forgot that was your house.' He was fairly sure he had not forgotten at the time. 'Can't you clear that away?'

'That's too heavy for me,' said Julie, trembling hand to trembling lip.

'Go and move it, now,' said Mum to Matthew.

'You said I wasn't to go there any more.'

'Well now I'm telling you you must go there. Get on with it.'

He followed Julie, stepping over Clive as he went.

Karen was sitting on the edge of the hole. When she heard them coming she set up a carefully modulated boo-hooing.

'You've spoilt our nice house,' she said.

Matthew didn't answer. He jumped down into the hole and threw out the rubbish. Julie stood over him with hands on hips until he had finished. He knew she was taking advantage of a situation she didn't understand, but this made it no less of an advantage.

'You've got to go back now,' she said, descending into the hole and pulling the roof into position. He could hear her voice drifting up through the corrugated iron. 'Don't do that, Karen. You'll get a disease.'

Mrs Harrison looked over the fence.

'Not digging today?'

'I've given that up,' said Matthew. 'You were right, there's nothing there.' Mrs Harrison failed to hear him.

'I told you there was nothing there,' she said. Hearing it twice in ten seconds was too much. He went down to the wall and watched Mrs Bagnall ranging the footpath and calling 'Minniminniminniminnimin!'

Mr Bagnall, on his side of the wall, was also watching.

'This is all very sad,' he said. 'I fear our Minnie may have met with an accident.'

'Everything's sad,' said Matthew.

Mr Bagnall looked thoughtful. 'Yes, you do seem to be *persona non grata* at the moment.'

'What's that?'

'Nobody loves you,' said Mr Bagnall. 'What happened?'

'I got into trouble at school,' said Matthew. 'Then I got into trouble at home because I'd been in trouble at school, and that was all because of the hole. Everyone thinks I've been fooling about. They wouldn't think that if I'd found anything.'

'You didn't find anything?'

'Just rubbish,' said Matthew. 'Chris and Paul said that wasn't rubbish. They said it would be archaeology in three thousand years' time if I left it there, but when they found something they took that away.'

'Can you face an unpalatable truth?' asked Mr Bagnall.

'What's that?'

'Something you won't like but ought to know. They were humouring you. Playing with the child to keep him happy, and amusing themselves at the same time. Not very kind but entirely understandable. You may feel like that yourself when you're older.'

'They weren't playing when they found the bottles,' said Matthew. 'The bottles were real antiques and they took them all. They wouldn't even let me keep one, and I needed that for school. That wouldn't have been so bad if I'd had something to show. I only kept digging because I thought I'd find things in the end. After you told me about Sir Oliver I was sure.'

'It was all my fault, was it?' said Mr Bagnall. Matthew thought he was offended but he stood there smiling with folded arms, turning himself into a skull and crossbones.

'I tried to get the bottles back,' said Matthew. 'I went all the way to Hoxenham by bus, and Paul gave me an old broken one and it got smashed. Then we had a row.'

'This has all come as rather a shock to me,' said Mr Bagnall. 'I thought you led such a quiet life. What did you row about?'

'I said something about his mother,' said Matthew, scraping at the wall with a bit of loose flint. 'I said no wonder she was never there, she must be sick of him.'

Mr Bagnall shook his head. 'That was bad.'

'I know that now,' said Matthew. 'But why? Nobody tells me, they just mutter. Is she dead?'

Mr Bagnall looked quickly at the house and then said, 'She left them, just after Easter. Did you really not know? Didn't you notice?'

Matthew had thought that things were so bad they couldn't possibly get any worse. Now he was in even rougher water.

'I thought she was away a lot, that's all. I didn't know she'd gone. I only wanted to make him angry: he kept smiling at me.'

'You did that all right,' said Mr Bagnall. 'You hit him in a very tender spot. Why on earth didn't you just hit him on the nose instead?'

'I didn't think,' said Matthew. 'I didn't know. What shall I do?' With the bit of flint he had engraved 'I HATE YOU' on one of the coping bricks. He didn't know who it was addressed to: perhaps to himself.

'Well don't cry, for a start,' said Mr Bagnall. 'And for God's sake don't go charging round there to apologize. That won't do any good.'

'But he's my friend,' said Matthew.

'Is he?'

'I thought he was going to be friends at first,' said Matthew.

'You aren't friends,' said Mr Bagnall. 'Be honest. You don't even like him.'

'He looks nice.'

'Of course he does,' said Mr Bagnall. 'He is nice. But that

doesn't mean you have to like him. I do, but why should you?'

'I don't seem to like anyone much,' said Matthew. 'No one likes me, either.'

'Clive does,' said Mr Bagnall, putting his hand over I HATE YOU. 'Look how he follows you about.'

'He only wants to dig.'

'No he doesn't, he wants you to play with him,' said Mr Bagnall. 'He thinks you're fantastic.'

'He's only a baby.'

'And what's he going to grow up into?' said Mr Bagnall, glumly. 'Good Lord, you've got a devoted admirer, there. Take care of him.'

'He's got Chris.'

'Would you like to be brought up by Chris?'

Clive, on the doorstep, felt that something was missing. The rubber band had gone. He must have swallowed it while he was being air horns. He dimly remembered Julie's threats about what rubber bands did when they got inside people and although he didn't know where his heart was, or even what it was, he knew what dead meant: the dull stiffening that turned a rat or a rabbit into a dirty rag in the ditch. Keeping very still, he felt the rubber band coiled like a wicked worm at the base of his throat.

He sat on the doorstep and waited to die.

Matthew, coming up the garden from the gap in the hedge, saw him crouched there, all drawn together with grief. Mum, on her way out with a basket of washing, stooped over him.

'Now whatever's the matter here?' she said, kneeling down.

Clive put his hands round his neck and whispered, 'That's gone.'

'What's gone?' said Mum. Clive opened his mouth.

'He's swallowed the band,' said Matthew.

'Has he?' said Mum. 'And what were they playing?'

'That was an elastic band,' said Matthew. 'He was chewing it and Julie said that would wind itself round his heart and kill him.'

Mum frowned at that and took Clive on her lap. 'Now listen to me, my man. That rubber band is down in your stomach along with your breakfast. That's all in little bits now. You won't die.'

Clive began to cry, because he was safe and because he was sorry for the band, all in bits and lost inside him. Mum lifted him up and carried him indoors to the biscuit tin.

'That Julie's a harpy,' she said.

'Julie's a harpy,' said Clive. It was a long sentence, for him. Matthew hoped he might try it again some time, when Julie was listening.

'Hang out that washing for me, will you,' said Mum. 'That's only your Dad's overalls.'

Matthew lowered the washing line on its pulley and pegged out the overalls. As he raised it again they filled with wind and bounced and bobbed against the sky, fat men playing hopscotch from cloud to cloud. The pulley squeaked in time to the bouncing, and Matthew became aware of another squeak from somewhere else; from the rubbish heap.

He went to look behind the withering flowers and cabbage stalks and potato peelings, and found the grass box from the lawn-mower that he had left there long ago, on the day that he had first begun the excavation. Inside it sat Minnie, suddenly grown thin. He bent down.

'Have you had your kittens, then?' he asked. Minnie climbed out of the grass box and leaned on him. At the bottom of the box were three little creatures, almost kittens, but only fur. He lifted them gently and they didn't move.

'Wait there, Minnie,' he said. The cat started to follow him and then went back to the grass box and sat beside it, looking at the kittens. Matthew took the laundry basket indoors. Mum was in the living-room with Clive so he went out again, closing the door without a sound. He returned to the rubbish heap, picked up Minnie, buttoned her into his jacket and tucked the grass box under his arm. Then he climbed over the wall to the Bagnalls' garden.

Mr Bagnall was sawing wood in his garage. When he noticed what Matthew was carrying he put down the saw and came to meet him.

'They're dead,' said Matthew. 'I found them just now. I'm sorry.'

Mr Bagnall looked at the kittens and then held out his hands for the cat. Matthew undid the buttons and handed Minnie over. Her ears were hot and she wailed, thinly.

'Oh, silly Min,' said Mr Bagnall, soothing her head. 'Why didn't you come home?' He ran his hands gently through her fur. 'No milk. She was too small to have kittens. Why didn't you come home?' he said again.

'Perhaps she was frightened,' said Matthew; then he looked at Minnie, clinging with all her claws to Mr Bagnall's coat, and saw what a ridiculous idea that was. He smiled at Mr Bagnall.

'It was a joke, wasn't it?'

'Not a very good joke,' said Mr Bagnall. 'But it amused us. Look, Matthew, would you mind burying them for me? I don't want Marge to see them.'

'I'll do it now,' said Matthew, and left with the grass box.

From the toolshed he fetched the little hand-fork and trowel that Mum used for weeding and went to make the grave. In a garden full of holes he didn't know where to make another. It had become a public garden: nowhere private, nowhere safe. In the end he went to the corner where the wall met Mrs Harrison's fence and the roots of the oak tree made secret caves. Under the most twisted root he dug the grave, too deep for night animals to disturb, and laid the kittens in it. Then he filled it again with earth and planted on top the house leeks that Chris had taken from the lean-to.

'They'll keep the lightning off,' he said.

'I see you've been digging again,' said Dad, at tea time.

'I haven't,' said Matthew.

'Well who have left the trowel and fork all muddy in the shed?'

'Oh, that sort of digging,' said Matthew. 'I was doing something for Mr Bagnall.'

'Fair enough,' said Dad. 'But go and clean them up before they rust. Your mum don't like her tools to be spoiled.'

It was almost dark outside. The toolshed was lit by a bright bulb that hung high, without a shade, among the spiders. Matthew took a stick and scraped the mud from the trowel. There was a stone jammed between the tines of the fork and when he forced it out with the point of the stick it fell on the concrete floor with a far-away clink. It rolled.

It was not a stone.

Matthew had to climb behind the lawn-mower to reach it. He held it under the light, rubbed away the dirt that clogged it, and burnished it on his sleeve. He was holding a ring, a black band that lay in his palm and defied the light. It looked as dark as lead but he felt no weight. It might be silver.

He rubbed it again on his coat and although it would not shine the surface became clear. On one side of the ring was a flat disc and on the disc was a figure, cut into the metal.

There was a sound outside. He stood still and clenched his hand over the ring, in case he was discovered, but no one came. A breeze seeped through the crack above the door and the shifting bulb set the shadows swinging against him. He made a pile of seed boxes in the middle of the floor and climbed on them to be nearer the light. The figure on the ring had a hair-line shadow of its own. To one who did not know it might have been nothing more than an idle scribble, accidental scratches, but Matthew knew exactly what it was; and the two curved lines beneath it might even be taken for a crescent moon.

He stood on his tottering tower of seed boxes and wondered what to do with it. It had come too late to save him, and after a while he was glad because there was no need to trade it for a good opinion.

He heard the sound again. Perhaps Mum in the kitchen or Dad in the garage. Perhaps someone putting down a tin pail and letting the handle drop. Matthew waited for the cold fear at his back, but it did not come. He slid the ring on to his finger and it fitted. Sir Oliver had been a small man with a slender hand.

He stood down from the boxes, opened the door, and looked into the night across the autumn garden.

'I'll wear that tonight,' said Matthew. 'And you can have it back tomorrow.'

The ring grew warm on his finger.

Thunder and Lightnings

Jan Mark

Victor knew more about aeroplanes than anyone Andrew
had ever met. His room was full of models and pictures.
His lamp was especially dimmed so that it looked like a
bomber's moon. Andrew was fascinated by Victor's
devotion to planes, but as their friendship grew, Andrew
became more and more worried about what would
happen to Victor when he discovered that his beloved
Lightnings were to be replaced by Jaguars . . .

A Pair of Desert-wellies

Sylvia Sherry

A vivid and enthralling story about a dare-devil
gangleader who cheeks everyone and lives by his wits.
Sequel to *A Pair of Jesus-boots*.

The Machine-gunners

Robert Westall

Chas McGill and friends build a nest for the German machine-gun Chas 'liberated'. And while they plan their own part in the war, the Tyneside authorities hunt for the lethal weapon. A Carnegie Medal winner.

The Butty Boy

Jill Paton Walsh

Harry is miserable to find that her new home is not by the seaside but deep in the countryside. So imagine her delight when she catches sight of a boat drifting past the garden fence – the next thing she knows, she's on board a horse-drawn narrow-boat with Ned the butty boy and his sister Bess, helping out as they make their slow journey along the canal carrying coal to the paper mill.

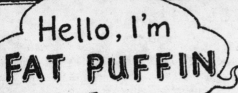